PRAISE FOR

THRESHOLD

"In Robinson's latest action fest, Jack Sigler, King of the Chess Team--a Delta Forces unit whose gonzo members take the names of chess pieces--tackles his most harrowing mission yet. Threshold elevates Robinson to the highest tier of over-the-top action authors and it delivers beyond the expectations even of his fans. The next Chess Team adventure cannot come fast enough."-- **Booklist - Starred Review**

"In Robinson's wildly inventive third Chess Team adventure (after Instinct), the U.S. president, Tom Duncan, joins the team in mortal combat against an unlikely but irresistible gang of enemies, including "regenerating capybara, Hydras, Neander-thals, [and] giant rock monsters." ...Video game on a page? Absolutely. Fast, furious unabashed fun? You bet." -- **Publishers Weekly**

"Jeremy Robinson's *Threshold* is one hell of a thriller, wildly imaginative and diabolical, which combines ancient legends and modern science into a non-stop action ride that will keep you turning the pages until the wee hours. Relentlessly gripping from start to finish, don't turn your back on this book!" -- **Douglas Preston, New York Times bestselling author of Impact and Blasphemy**

"With *Threshold* Jeremy Robinson goes pedal to the metal into very dark territory. Fast-paced, action-packed and wonderfully creepy! Highly recommended!" -- **Jonathan Maberry, *New York Times* bestselling author of *The King of Plagues* and *Rot & Ruin***

"*Threshold* is a blisteringly original tale that blends the thriller and horror genres in a smooth and satisfying hybrid mix. With his new entry in the Jack Sigler series, Jeremy Robinson plants his feet firmly on territory blazed by David Morrell and James Rollins. The perfect blend of mysticism and monsters, both human and otherwise, make *Threshold* as groundbreaking as it is riveting." -- **Jon Land**, *New York Times* bestselling author of *Strong Enough to Die*

"Jeremy Robinson is the next James Rollins."-- **Chris Kuzneski, New York Times bestselling author of The Lost Throne and The Prophecy**

"Jeremy Robinson's *Threshold* sets a blistering pace from the very first page and never lets up. This globe-trotting thrill ride challenges its well-crafted heroes with ancient mysteries, fantastic creatures, and epic action sequences. For readers seeking a fun rip-roaring adventure, look no further."
-- **Boyd Morrison, bestselling author of** *The Ark*

"Robinson artfully weaves the modern day military with ancient history like no one else."-- **Dead Robot Society**

"THRESHOLD is absolutely gripping. A truly unique story mixed in with creatures and legendary figures of mythology, technology and more fast-paced action than a Jerry Bruckheimer movie. If you want fast-paced: you got it. If you want action: you got it. If you want mystery: you got it, and if you want intrigue, well, you get the idea. In short, I $@#!$% loved this one."-- **thenovelblog.com**

"As always the Chess Team is over the top of the stratosphere, but anyone who relishes an action urban fantasy thriller that combines science and mythology will want to join them for the exhilarating Pulse pumping ride."-- **Genre Go Round Reviews**

INSTINCT

"If you like thrillers original, unpredictable and chock-full of action, you are going to love Jeremy Robinson's Chess Team. INSTINCT riveted me to my chair." -- **Stephen Coonts, NY Times bestselling author of THE DISCIPLE and DEEP BLACK: ARCTIC GOLD**

"Robinson's slam-bang second Chess Team thriller [is a] a wildly inventive yarn that reads as well on the page as it would play on a computer screen."-- **Publisher's Weekly**

"Intense and full of riveting plot twists, it is Robinson's best book yet, and it should secure a place for the Chess Team on the A-list of thriller fans who like the over-the-top style of James Rollins and Matthew Reilly." -- **Booklist**

"Jeremy Robinson is a fresh new face in adventure writing and will make a mark in suspense for years to come." -- **David Lynn Golemon, NY Times bestselling author of LEGEND and EVENT**

"Instinct is a jungle fever of raw adrenaline that goes straight for the jugular."-- **Thomas Greanias, NY Times bestselling author of THE ATLANTIS PROPHECY and THE PROMISED WAR**

PULSE

"Robinson's latest reads like a video game with tons of action and lots of carnage. The combination of mythology, technology, and high-octane action proves irresistible. Gruesome and nasty in a good way, this will appeal to readers of Matthew Reilly." -- **Booklist**

"Raiders of the Lost Arc meets Tom Clancy meets Saturday matinee monster flick with myths, monsters, special ops supermen and more high tech weapons than a Bond flick. Pulse is an over-the-top, bullet-ridden good time." -- **Scott Sigler, New York Times bestselling author of CONTAGIOUS and INFECTED**

"Jeremy Robinson's latest novel, PULSE, ratchets his writing to the next level. Rocket-boosted action, brilliant speculation, and the recreation of a horror out of the mythologic past, all seamlessly blend into a rollercoaster ride of suspense and adventure. Who knew chess could be this much fun!" -- **James Rollins, New York Times bestselling author of THE LAST ORACLE**

PULSE contains all of the danger, treachery, and action a reader could wish for. Its band of heroes are gutsy and gritty. Jeremy Robinson has one wild imagination, slicing and stitching his tale together with the deft hand of a surgeon. Robinson's impressive talent is on full display in this one." -- **Steve Berry, New York Times bestselling author of THE CHARLE-MAGNE PURSUIT**

" Jeremy Robinson dares to craft old-fashioned guilty pleasures - far horizons, ancient maps, and classic monsters - hardwired for the 21st century. There's nothing timid about Robinson as he drops his readers off the cliff without a parachute and somehow manages to catch us an inch or two from doom." -- **Jeff Long, New York Times bestselling author of THE DESCENT and YEAR ZERO**

CALLSIGN: KING

UNDERWORLD

JEREMY ROBINSON

WITH SEAN ELLIS

BREAKNECK MEDIA

Visit Jeremy Robinson on the World Wide Web at:
www.jeremyrobinsononline.com

Visit Sean Ellis on the World Wide Web at:
seanellisthrillers.webs.com

FICTION BY JEREMY ROBINSON

The Jack Sigler Thrillers
Threshold
Instinct
Pulse

Callsign: King – Book 1
Callsign: Queen – Book 1
Callsign: Rook – Book 1
Callsign: Bishop – Book 1
Callsign: Knight – Book 1

The Antarktos Saga
The Last Hunter – Descent
The Last Hunter – Pursuit
The Last Hunter – Ascent

Origins Editions (first five novels)
Kronos
Antarktos Rising
Beneath
Raising the Past
The Didymus Contingency

Writing as Jeremy Bishop
Torment
The Sentinel

Short Stories
Insomnia

Humor
The Zombie's Way (Ike Onsoomyu)
The Ninja's Path (Kutyuso Deep)

FICTION BY SEAN ELLIS

CALLSIGN:
KING
UNDERWORLD

1049 UTC

Status report requested.

>>>It's over. King is dead.

PROLOGUE

An unknown land — c. 400 BCE

The man paused at the mouth of cave and peered into its
shadowy depths. A foul odor wafted up from hole in the world,
riding on wisps of gray steam. He knew the common people
living nearby believed the steam to be the mephitic vapors,
rising from the decaying corpse of *Typhoeus*, the dragon slain by
Zeus in his war with the Titans and buried in the heart of the
Earth. They were the same vapors that supposedly gave the
sibylline oracles the gift of prophecy. But he knew better. The
gods, the stories surrounding them and the tales of his own
heroic quests were primarily fictions created to misdirect the
populace from the truth.

Granted, there were many strange things in the world, but
with the proper amount of study, the secrets of nature could be
revealed, and used to boost physical strength, extend life, heal
the body and he believed, travel great distances in the blink of
an eye. To the undisciplined mind, these secrets were magical.
Godlike even. Which led to his current status as the bastard son
of Zeus. The title afforded him access to every possible resource

he needed, including a long voyage he took with the crew of the Argo around the world and back.

But the real benefit of his demigod status was that every strange encounter or event was quickly reported to him. Man's fear of the unknown sent them racing to the man-god so that he might continue his "labors" and expunge the evil, which frequently turned out to be a harmless, previously unknown animal species or atmospheric event. But everywhere he went, people came to him with pleas for help. His height, muscular body and curly brown hair made him easily identifiable and would eventually become a problem. His need for secrecy meant he'd eventually have to disappear and let future generations believe him a myth, but for now he would use his position to find the answers he sought.

He rooted in his pack for a torch. The oil soaked brand took the spark from his flint, and he waved it over the mouth of the cave experimentally. Sometimes, vapors like these had a way of igniting so that the air itself burned; this time, it did not. Satisfied with the precaution, he began his descent into the pit.

This most recent "labor" had been brought to his attention just days ago. He'd nearly ignored the story, but curiosity got the better of him. His own imagination was the source for many of the current religious beliefs, spread dutifully by his band of followers who knew only half the truth. He'd conjured stories of the Underworld, driving a fear of the subterranean world into the hearts of men, because that's where he conducted his work and hid his secrets. But if the story of missing children and cave dwelling creatures was to be believed, his fictions had stumbled upon a grain of truth.

He hefted his club onto one shoulder and patted the wine-skin tied to his waist. The fluid it contained would give him the strength to overcome any obstacle he came across. Satisfied that he was prepared, he moved onward.

How far down he went into the eternal darkness, he could not say. To his tired feet, which rolled and slipped as his sandals trod the irregular surface, it felt as if he had walked perhaps three or four *schoinos*—a journey that might take an ordinary man a full day. But he had only burned through two of his torches, which meant that he had been in the cave perhaps only an hour or two. In that time, he saw no other living creatures, but he sensed their presence often, and he knew that they had seen him. Further on, he found their spoor—not only their excrement, but also castoff bits of wood and metal, even scraps of cloth, which had somehow found their way down from the surface. It was not long before he began to recognize the detritus for what it was: the trappings of a funeral. This was indeed, the land of the dead.

He soon came to an underground river. One of the three children who wandered into this cave had managed to escape. He told a story of a river and of horrible monsters that had taken his two sisters.

The child's story proved accurate. One of the denizens of the Underworld, which did not flee at the first glimmer of torchlight, stood before him. The creature he now beheld looked like nothing like nothing he'd encountered before.

It might have once been human. The hairless body had the shape of a man—two arms, two legs, one head with the right number of eyes and other orifices, no tail—but that by itself meant little. If it—he—had been a man, perhaps driven into the heart of the Earth by madness, then somewhere along the way he had suffered grievous injury; the gaunt body was misshapen and twisted, as if every one of its extremities had been broken and then allowed to heal improperly.

The creature sat on its haunches, bent over and engaged in some task that completely held its attention. It raised its head, gazing at the strange shadows cast by the flickering flame of the warrior's torch, but then immediately went back to what it was doing.

The man advanced, curious about the creature's activity. He saw a foot, then its match...legs, small and pale...a supine child. One of the two missing girls. Was the creature feasting on the girl? While others would feel revolt and rage, the man felt only curiosity.

He stepped closer and drew back his club, in case the creature attacked, but the motion startled the creature. It scampered away, and before the man could catch it, the beast was hopping across the river. Its feet made hardly a splash, as if it was walking on the surface of the water, and a moment later, it stood on the far bank, hissing angrily at the trespasser.

The man inspected the child and saw right away that his assumption was incorrect. The child's body hadn't been gnawed on, but she *had* been killed and.... He stepped closer, looking at her head. The girl's hair—all of it—was missing. She'd been scalped. But not recently. He could see by the condition of her body that she'd been dead for some time. The creature had not been eating her flesh, but rather had been tending to the remains. He saw now that the girl's body rested on a bier of wood, as if in preparation for an offering...no, it was a raft.

Inspiration struck. *I'll call him the ferryman, and this will be the river, Styx—the path to Hades.* He'd conjured tales of Hades long ago, basing the hellish place on stories from older religions. But details like this, based on fact, would help reinforce mankind's fear of the Underworld.

The man relaxed, letting his club fall back against his shoulder. He moved away from the child and walked to the edge of the river. The creature hunched its shoulders angrily, glowering at him, but it left off its keening wail.

The river was deeper than he expected. He could see the water, a few cubits below, along the almost vertical stone bank, but the bed was hidden from his eyes. A few rocks protruded from the surface, some barely rising above the flow, others stabbing up as high as he was tall.

That was how the creature had crossed the river; stepping stones formed a path across, a secret way known only to the ferryman.

The man knelt at the edge and cautiously touched the surface of the water with a fingertip. He could feel the gentle tug of the current, but after a moment, something else. *Burning.* It was not heat, as from a fire, but the sting of a laundryman's lye. He drew his finger back quickly, and saw the calloused skin already starting to peel away.

Not even he could swim across the Styx.

The man stood, contemplating the river and his destination, which lay on the other side, across the secret path known only to ferryman. He waved the torch over the water, studying the way the water rippled around the stones hidden just out of view. Perhaps through trial and error, he could find the correct path, but one slip…

No. There had to be another way.

He glanced down at the girl, so serene in death, eyes closed as if merely asleep, mouth open ever so slightly as if to draw a breath.

Then the man glimpsed the faint reflection of torchlight on something in the child's mouth and he understood what he needed to do.

He took the leather *kibisis* from his belt and dug out two tarnished silver *tetradrachm* coins, which he held up for the creature to see. The thing bared its hideous teeth at him—the man realized it was a grin of satisfaction—and it nimbly forded the river once more.

He paid careful attention to where it stepped, memorizing the safe path—*yes*, he thought. *I can do this.* Then the thing was standing expectantly before him, hand outstretched.

The man dropped the two coins onto the creature's open palm.

He heaved the club onto his shoulder once more, and followed the creature across the river, with only the soles of his sandals dipping into the alkaline water, as he leapt between the crossing stones.

As he set off along the far shore, resuming his exploration, he got a last glimpse of the creature hugging the offering of coins to its chest. The price for passage into the Underworld had been paid. Whether the man could find his way back out was none of the ferryman's concern.

East of Phoenix, Arizona — Yesterday — 2053 UTC (1:53 pm Local)

The smartphone on the passenger seat of the Nissan Altima chirped and Leilani Rhodes glanced over to see who had sent the text message. "Becca. What now?"

She picked up the phone and held it against the steering wheel as she tapped the touchscreen to display the message. She glanced down quickly to read it, then made a little growling noise in the back of her throat. "Seriously?"

The screen read:

I think im going to cut my hair

Leilani turned her eyes back to the road ahead. It would have been easy enough to reply; the section of US Highway 60 through which she now drove was almost completely straight for at least another ten miles, and the only vehicle she could see was an eighteen-wheeler a good mile ahead of her—she'd probably catch up and pass him in the next few minutes. But the truth of the matter was that she didn't want to reply to Becca's inane message. Becca was a good friend, but oh so needy, and Leilani just didn't want to deal with that right now.

Especially not right this instant, driving on the remote highway between her home in Globe and her job in Mesa. She hated the drive, hated living in Globe and hated the job, all of which meant she was in a foul mood to begin with, and not at all sympathetic to Becca's grooming crisis.

The phone chirped again in her hand.

Shuold i????

Leilani had lived her life—all 22 years of it—in the Arizona town some sixty miles from the edge of the Phoenix metro area. As a teenager, she had chafed at the limitations of the remote location; Phoenix, with its malls and marginally hipper scene, was just too far away. Getting her first car hadn't helped much, because while the distance separating Globe from the city was relatively short, it required a sojourn through some of the most desolate terrain in the United States. Blisteringly hot asphalt, undulating mountains where lightning and even hail storms could descend at a moments notice, the possibility of overheating from using the air conditioner—and you couldn't *not* use it—or a flat from one of the ubiquitous chunks of disintegrating truck tires scattered like land mines on the roadway, were just a few of the factors that gave the trip nightmare potential.

After finishing high school, she had enrolled at ASU, but living closer to the city, on campus, was about the only thing about college she had found appealing. So after just two semesters, she had dropped out and moved back home. The derailment of her plans for higher education had brought her face to face with the harsh realities of adult life; she had been unable to find work—at least the kind of work she was willing to do—in her hometown. After a few months, she had started looking in the city, even though it meant a daily commute through the wasteland. Her plan had been to get a job, and then with a few paychecks under her belt, find a place to live in Phoenix.

Six months later, she was still making the drive, four days a week, to her job at a sports bar in Mesa. Even though she lived frugally, at least by her own estimation, something always seemed to come up to drain away her savings before she could make the move.

Now, she wasn't just sick of living in Globe. She was sick of the desert altogether.

Chirp.

Well??????

Leilani glanced down at the touch screen keyboard on the phone just long enough to tap out:

>>>Driving!!!

When her eyes met the road again, it was like looking at the end of the world.

So many things were happening at once, her brain couldn't process all the incoming visual stimuli.

Directly ahead of her, the eighteen-wheeler was sideways, its white trailer stretching across both lanes, and relative to Leilani in her Altima, it was coming up fast. All around the trailer there was black smoke and dust, and pieces of debris were flying through the air from beyond it. There were flashes to the north, a veritable strobe of lightning, stabbing down out of a clear sky. And all along the roadside, there was movement: dark shapes that looked almost like people, swarming down from the hills.

She stomped her foot on the brake pedal, but as adrenaline slammed through her body, leaving her extremities strangely numb, she knew she wasn't going to be able to stop in time. The semi's trailer slowly rolled over directly in front of her as the Altima's anti-lock brakes peeled away the car's momentum…seventy-five to fifty in the space of a heartbeat…the underside of the trailer looming ahead of her like a monolith…fifty to thirty…

Damn you, Becca. I'm going to die because you couldn't make up your own mind about a haircut.

The Altima was still moving forward at about twenty miles per hour when its front end crunched into the obstacle. To Leilani, everything seemed to be happening in slow motion, but her responses were entirely reflexive—disconnected from any conscious decisions. She tightened her grip on the steering wheel…felt the phone slip from her grasp as she did…and then she was thrown forward. The airbag exploded from the steering column, protecting her from impact even as it showered her in a fine spray of pyrotechnic residue. She rebounded from the safety cushion, and was surprised by the fact that, except for a throbbing pain across her collarbone, where her seatbelt had locked in place to restrain her during impact, she was unhurt.

A wave of sublime joy washed over her, cleaning away the terror of the preceding moment. She was alive and that was unexpected. But her transcendent happiness was fleeting. A glance across the rapidly deflating airbag revealed the aftermath of the crash; the front end of the Altima looked like an accordion, crumpled beyond recognition, and steam was hissing from the destroyed radiator.

Oh, my god. It's totaled, Leilani thought. *How am I going to pay for this?*

Such mundane thoughts ricocheted through her head, transforming the miracle of her survival into something onerous, but this too was a temporary reaction. She pushed down the rising despair as a more rational part of her brain realized that the crisis was not over.

The phone had been knocked from her hand by the airbag, and as she tried to pick it up, she found that her hands were trembling. Just closing her fingers on the slim plastic case was like trying to thread a needle. She finally got a grip on it and brought it up from the floor, but as soon as she tapped in 9-1-1, she saw the words "No Service" flash across the display.

"What is this, the 90's?" she muttered. Leilani couldn't remember ever not being able to get coverage. She directed a few choice curse words at her wireless service, but the message did not change.

"Well, what good are you, anyway?" she finally said to the phone. Then it occurred to her that it was more than just a phone.

She activated the video camera function and then held it out in front of her, framing the crash scene in the phone's display. "Okay," she said, haltingly at first. "I was just in a huge accident. A semi flipped over right in front of me, and I couldn't stop in time. There's also some weird shit going on out in the desert. A lot of lightning… I wonder if that's why I can't get a signal?"

She aimed the phone toward the mountains on her right, catching several flashes at an oblique angle. "Anyway, it's pretty weird. I think I'll get out and take a look around."

As she said it, it occurred to her for the first time that the driver of the eighteen-wheeler might be injured…or worse. Somehow, that made the idea of shooting video of the crash seem more than just silly; it was almost ghoulish.

She depressed the button on her seatbelt, but it refused to release. "Damn it. Doesn't anything work?"

Suddenly, something slammed against the window beside her. A sound like a gunshot reverberated through the vehicle, startling her and opening the adrenaline gates once more. She tried to pull away instinctively even as she snapped her head around to get a look, but the seat belt held her fast.

A nightmare gazed through the window at her. It was a man...except it wasn't a man; it wasn't even human. It was the face of a demon.

The thing's baleful red eyes fixed on Leilani, and it bared its teeth in a feral snarl as it hammered its hairy fists against the glass again.

Primal panic tore through Leilani, as she struggled in vain to loosen the seat belt. She didn't even bother with the latch, but instead slipped her upper torso under the shoulder strap, giving the belt enough slack to allow her to squirm snake-like out of its restraining embrace.

The creature pounded again, and the Altima shook under the assault.

Leilani half-rolled over the center divider, but the seat belt caught on her shoes. She struggled and kicked, and when that didn't work she tried slipping the shoes off.

The car shuddered again, the impact so ferocious that Leilani pitched forward, into the foot well on the passenger side. She tried to push herself up but her arms were pinned beneath her and every inch of movement was a titanic struggle, made all the more impossible by the relentless shaking.

There was a harsh snapping sound as the driver's side window broke under the furious hammering, transforming instantly into an opaque mosaic of tiny tempered glass particles, held together only by a thin laminate coating, and then the curtain separating her from the demon fell apart as the creature thrust both arms through.

Leilani felt its fingers graze her leg and somehow found the will to wrestle her arms free and push herself off the floor. She stretched a hand out for the passenger's side armrest, felt her fingers close on the latch lever, and frantically pulled at it. There was a click inside the door panel as the mechanism released. She threw the door open, and with a near-superhuman effort, heaved herself through the opening.

She felt the creature's nails rake the bare skin of her leg, but that minor injury was nothing to what she experienced when she crashed face first onto the hot asphalt alongside the wrecked Altima. Both hurts however were muted by the anaesthetizing flood of endorphins. The scrapes and bruises might as well have been happening to someone else for all that she felt them. A single imperative drove her now.

Run!

She scrabbled for a purchase on the blisteringly hot tar macadam and pulled herself the rest of the way out of the car. She was on her feet an instant later and immediately started moving.

She didn't get far.

Another demon appeared from behind the rear of the Altima, blocking her escape. The thing rose to full height, towering over her, all matted black hair, carious yellow teeth and bloody red eyes. She pivoted, trying to get around it, ducking under the sweep of its massive arms, but before she could move, she felt the ground slip away. Another pair of arms seized her from behind and closed tight in a crushing embrace.

There was just enough air in her lungs for a scream.

2122 UTC (2:22 pm Local)

Arizona Department of Public Safety officer Matt Becker felt a moment of dread as he stopped his police cruiser and stepped out of its air-conditioned environs into the desert heat. He'd seen plenty of carnage on the road in his six years with DPS, and it never got any easier. According to the 911 call, this one was probably going to be pretty bad, but it was what he was paid to do.

Traffic coming from Phoenix was already piling up on 60. From what he could tell, the wreck was at least twenty minutes old, but no one from the long queue of idling vehicles had ventured out to play Good Samaritan. That was probably for the best, but Becker thought it a little strange; usually there was always someone eager to offer their services or at the very least, gawk at the twisted bodies. Today however, the onlookers seemed to want to keep a healthy distance; there was a gap of almost half-a-mile between the first stopped car—presumably the person who had placed the emergency call—and the edge of the wreck.

Becker left the cruiser with its MARS lights flashing a constant warning, and jogged toward the chaotic sculpture of fiberglass and metal. It was difficult to tell how many vehicles were actually involved. There were three eighteen-wheelers, all of them either jack-knifed or on their side, but pieces of passenger cars and SUVs poked out from beneath them. Becker counted at least six different smaller vehicles. Yet, it was only as he was completing his hasty assessment of the wreck that he realized something was profoundly wrong.

There wasn't a soul in sight.

It was extremely rare to find a rollover accident where passengers weren't ejected on impact. Seat belts weren't always a sure way to prevent being thrown when a car traveling close to eighty miles an hour suddenly started tumbling, and statistically, there were always a few dumb schmucks who couldn't be bothered to "click it." This time however, there were no scattered bodies. Nor were there any walking wounded, milling about the site in a state of shock.

Shaking his head, Becker approached the nearest vehicle—the rear end of a silver Ford Taurus, was poking out from under the tanker-trailer of a big rig—and stuck his head in through the sprung left rear door. Through the almost overpowering smell of evaporating gasoline and diesel, he caught the metallic odor of blood. Red-black streaks and clumps of gory tissue painted the interior, but there were no bodies.

Becker felt a chill creep down his back in defiance of the Sonoran Desert heat. He moved over to the nearby semi and peered in through the spider-webbed windshield.

No one there.

"What the—?"

Becker's disbelief gave way to trepidation as he moved into the heart of the pile-up, but there was not a single person, living or dead, in the entire tableau. Only blood, sometimes in copious amounts, splattering the interiors of the wrecks and drying to black spots on the asphalt, offered any sort of proof that the occupants of the vehicles had not been simply whisked away, raptured off to heaven or beamed up onto an orbiting alien starship.

No, Becker thought. *People died here. And then someone took them.*

He kept searching, but his initial eagerness had given way to funereal dread. On the far edge of the pile-up, he found one last vehicle, a dark blue Nissan Altima that had slammed into the underside of an overturned shipping container, which stretched across the road like a gate. He glanced up the highway and saw that, here too, a surreal buffer zone existed between the wreck and the line of traffic from the east.

Becker circled the Altima, knowing full well that there would be no body, but then something caught his eye and he stuck his head in through the opening where the driver's side window had been.

Lying on the floor, covered in tiny particles of broken glass, was a smartphone.

He picked it up and swiped a gloved thumb across the display to wake the device. The screen immediately lit up and showed a live-action image of the interior of the car; the video-camera function was actively recording.

"Holy shit," he breathed. Someone had been shooting footage of the accident, and Becker realized that the answer to the bizarre disappearance might literally be in the palm of his hand.

He tapped at the 'stop' button, and saw a menu pop-up on the screen.

Upload video? [YES] [NO]

He tried to stab at the "no" button, but his gloved fingertip must have dragged across the alternative, because the menu changed to a progress bar that quickly registered "100%" and then flashed the message:

File Uploaded

"Crap." Becker stripped off his right glove, knowing full well that it was a serious break in procedure, and with far more dexterity, he navigated through the phone's files to locate the video segment by its timestamp. He tapped on the file icon and the display switched to a view of the crumpled front end of the Altima, as viewed from the driver's seat.

Becker watched and listened with rapt attention as the Altima's occupant—a young woman by the sound of her voice—recorded the aftermath of the experience.

Then something unbelievable happened.

After six years with DPS, Matt Becker thought he'd seen it all, but he had never seen anything like this.

EXCLUSION

1.

New York City — 1335 UTC (9:35 am Local)

George Pierce stared at the person sitting in the threadbare easy chair with a mixture of pity, revulsion and disbelief. When the man smiled, revealing missing and decayed teeth, the proportions remained about the same, but the emotional brew roiling in his gut spilled over like beer from a shaken bottle.

"George," the man said, his voice grateful, but with an undercurrent that made Pierce wary. "Long time, brother."

You aren't my brother, Pierce wanted to say. *You're someone who happens to share some genetic material with me, but you sold your right to call me 'brother' for an eight-ball, and shot up, snorted, smoked…or whatever the hell it is you do with that crap. You burned that bridge a long time ago. My real brother is sitting downstairs, waiting for me.*

But he didn't say that or anything like it. Instead, he managed a weak smile and sat down. "Hey, Micah."

"I'm glad you came," Micah Pierce said. He nodded his head enthusiastically, but to George Pierce, it looked almost like an involuntary nervous tic. "I feel good about this. I think I'm really going to be able to kick it this time."

Pierce also felt his head bobbing, but the confident utterance made no impression whatsoever. Micah was reading from an old script; they had played this scene out four times, *was it? Five? I've lost track*, Pierce thought.

The first time, Pierce had been wholeheartedly supportive of his sibling's declared intent to end his narcotics addition. He had taken a leave of absence from his position at the University of Athens, effectively ceding control of a very important research project to one of his colleagues and along with it, the credit for the subsequent discovery, to give Micah his unconditional emotional support during the weeks of rehab and his subsequent effort to get established in society.

The second time, almost eighteen months later, Pierce had been more cautious, but still hopeful. Relapses happened, but Micah was family—his only remaining blood relative.

Micah's second "clean" period, or rather the length of time between the end of his stint in rehab and his arrest for attempting to sell stolen property, which led to another court-ordered stay at an addiction treatment facility, had lasted only four months.

Pierce no longer felt any hope when Micah emerged from his personal darkness with another promise to throw the monkey off his back once and for all. Pierce felt only a profound weariness, and no small measure of guilt, partly because of his perceived failure to do the impossible and somehow lift his brother up, but mostly because he just wanted Micah to stop calling.

He nodded perfunctorily at Micah's assurances, and chimed in with as few words as possible when his younger brother began reminiscing about experiences from their childhood—memories that were so colored and distorted as to bear little resemblance to anything that had really occurred. Pierce did not attempt to set the record straight. He had read a lot of literature about addiction over the years and recognized the classic behavior of an incorrigible addict.

On an earlier occasion, armed with academic knowledge, Pierce had confronted his brother with these realities, reducing Micah to tears, but in the end, it hadn't made any difference. Now, Pierce no longer bothered.

He still took Micah's calls and came to visit him when he made an apparent effort to get clean, but it wasn't because he entertained hope that things would change. He came because he knew that someday, maybe someday soon, Micah would wind up on a slab, and then Pierce would really feel guilty. He didn't want his last interaction with his only blood relative to be one of abject rejection.

When he could take no more of it, he rose. "Mike, I can't stay."

The younger Pierce started to protest, but George headed him off. "I think you really can do it this time if you want it bad enough." He leaned over and gave Micah a quick perfunctory hug, then hastened out of the room without another word.

As he moved down the short hallway to the stairs, Pierce felt like he was struggling to breathe in a vacuum. The visit with Micah had sucked the energy right out of him, and he desperately needed to get away. He was almost running as he reached the door to the lobby, and tapped his foot anxiously as he waited for the receptionist to release the electronic lock, permitting him to rejoin the man he thought of as his true brother. He caught sight of the tall, athletic-looking figure in faded jeans and a black Elvis T-shirt, standing pensively near the exit.

"That's done," Pierce said. "Now let's head upstate where I can get some of the stink off…"

Pierce's voice trailed away as he noticed the other man's urgent expression. "Uh, oh. I know that look. Let me guess: duty calls?"

The other man returned a grim smile and held up his smartphone as if that explained everything—it did. "I'm going to need you on this one."

2.

Ivan Sokoloff peered through the EO Tech Gen II 3X scope at the front door of the innocuous looking brownstone residence, and waited. When the door opened, as he expected it to in the next few minutes, he would become ten million dollars richer. He let his finger brush the trigger of the bolt-action Remington Model 700 and felt an unexpected stir of anticipation; it felt surprisingly good to be working again.

Sokoloff had thought he was done with this life, and up until only a month ago, he had considered himself happily retired. Like anyone who enjoys their work, there had been some moments of ennui at the prospect of giving up his lucrative career, but it had been a necessary thing. His success in his chosen profession had become a liability; too many people knew of him, knew his deadly reputation, and it was inevitable that he would eventually, having lived by the sword, also die by it. Perhaps it would be a bloody showdown with law enforcement agents or an unexpected betrayal from one of his own associates, hoping to cement a reputation by being the man who killed the world's deadliest hitman. Or it would just be that his luck would run out—one job too many, his reflexes no longer quite as quick as they once were, his target just a little too well defended.

That was how nearly all professional killers ended their careers, and for a long time, Sokoloff was resigned to that eventuality. But the longer he stayed alive, notching one successful job after another, building a tremendous personal fortune secreted away in various untraceable bank accounts, he had begun to realize that he didn't really want to go out in a blaze of glory. There was, after all, something to be said for the living the good life and dying at a ripe old age in a lavish cabana in the tropics.

Of course, it wasn't as simple as giving two weeks notice and walking away. Even retired, he would still have been a very desirable target for any number of enemies. The only way to truly close the door on his past life was to end it, literally. He had to die, or rather make the world believe that he was dead.

Planning his own "murder" hadn't been terribly difficult. He had found a suitable body double—a homeless man who would never be missed—and strangled him to death, leaving the body in a villa in Greece, along with just enough physical evidence to sell the deception. With the right bribes, he had seen to it that no autopsy was conducted before the body was cremated, and while rumors persisted for sometime thereafter that Sokoloff had faked his death, his complete disappearance from that world had eventually quieted those suspicions. After all, who would believe that the deadliest professional killer in the world had simply chosen to give up his exciting lifestyle to sip fruity tropical drinks and work on his tan?

Yet, that was exactly what he had done, and aside from an occasional wistful moment, he had done it very well for more than a decade. That was perhaps why he had felt nothing but dread when, while lounging by his pool four short weeks earlier, he had received a cryptic text message.

He had glanced at the phone's display with almost casual indifference, imagining that it was an invitation to dinner at the casino or something equally mundane, but to his consternation, he saw that the sender was "unknown." The message said simply:

$1,000,000 (US) deposited to your bank account (XXXXXX833). Confirm and await further communication.

Sokoloff had felt as if someone had just walked across his grave. *Someone is probing me. Ignore it. Don't take the bait.*

A few seconds later, the phone had vibrated again.

This amount is a deposit to secure your services. Please confirm promptly.

Sokoloff's heart had begun hammering in his chest. He had not felt such fear, such a sense of imminent danger, in so long, his body had lost its immunity to adrenaline. For a moment, he had considered hurling the phone into the pool. Before he could act on that impulse however, the phone shivered in his hands.

Exactly sixty seconds from the receipt of this message, international law enforcement agencies will be notified of your location and supplied with the identification numbers for all six of your bank accounts. Your assets will be frozen immediately.

Another message arrived even as the first was driving through his head like a railroad spike.

There is a 63.2% probability that your arrest and/or termination will follow within 24 hours. To prevent this, please confirm receipt of $1,000,000 US as retainer for your services. You now have approximately 45 seconds.

With trembling hands, Sokoloff had pounded out a terse reply:

>>>Who teh hell is ths?

The answer had come almost immediately.

Automatic notification of law enforcement agencies suspended for the moment. Please confirm deposit to your bank account.

The money had been there, as promised, and even though he had more than enough to last him the rest of his life, he still goggled in disbelief at the updated account balance. No sooner had he logged off from the bank than another message arrived.

Your services are required. Upon fulfillment of the contract, you will receive $10,000,000 (US).

>>>You obviously know who I am, but I am retired. I don't do that anymore.

Your unique skill set and high degree of personal motivation, in conjunction with the resources that will be made available to you, ensures the highest degree of probability for successful fulfillment of the contract. A secure communication device will arrive shortly. Stand by for further instructions.

An hour later, he had signed for a parcel delivery. The package had contained only an ordinary looking smart phone, sent from an address in France two days earlier. As soon as he had powered it up, the electronic conversation had begun in earnest.

The target was a man named Jack Sigler, but his employer chose to utilize the code name "King." King, he was told, was in all likelihood, a covert special operations soldier for the US Army. A concerted effort had been made to erase all evidence of

Sigler from the public record. The only picture of him that Sokoloff's anonymous new employer could provide was from a courthouse video surveillance camera—King had participated in a child custody hearing and his image had been captured as he left the building. Nothing was known about his current whereabouts, but Sokoloff's contact had amassed a great deal of unofficial information about the man, including King's close friendship with an archaeologist named George Pierce.

Pierce, Sokoloff realized, would be the key to executing the contract, and unlike King, the archaeologist's life was an open book.

It had taken nearly three weeks to put all the pieces in place. Pierce's drug-addicted brother had been located in New York City, and it hadn't been too difficult to arrange for his arrest on a completely valid charge of petty larceny, or to subsequently see that he was sent to a court-ordered stay at a rehabilitation facility. Sokoloff knew that Micah Pierce would reach out to his brother, and the elder Pierce would probably make contact with Sigler. Sokoloff had been right on both counts. Shortly after the call from his brother, Pierce had made an untraceable phone call to someone in the United States, and thereafter booked a flight from Athens to New York.

Armed only with a grainy picture of the target, Sokoloff had stationed himself at the reception area of La Guardia Airport, awaiting the arrival of Pierce's plane. King had been there as well.

Sokoloff probably could have pulled off the hit right there, outside the secure terminal, but the risk of immediate capture was too great. He had brought the target into the open and he had gone to great lengths to set up the ambush at the rehab clinic; as eager as he was to be done with this one last job, he wasn't about to throw ten million dollars away—to say nothing of his own freedom—with an impetuous act. So instead, he had followed Pierce and King through the city to the brownstone where Micah Pierce, having already played his role—albeit unknowingly, waited for a reunion with his older brother. While that was going on, Sokoloff had gotten in position on a rooftop across the street, deploying the Remington he'd purchased at an upstate sporting goods store earlier in the week. Then he made a call to his local connection.

He had no doubt of his ability to end Sigler's life with a single pull of the trigger, unaided by any reinforcements. He was likewise certain of his ability to slip away unhindered. But bringing in members of the local Russian organized crime syndicate would add a layer of protection to the job that would completely deflect all suspicion from himself, and perhaps more importantly, from his employer. At his signal, the locals would stage a very public, very visible attack on the clinic, and the ensuing confusion would lead authorities to believe that King was simply a victim of bad timing. They would eventually realize that the fatal bullet had come from a high-powered rifle, and not from the pistols or sub-machine guns wielded by local mob foot soldiers, but that would be a mere detail. The shooters would be arrested and sent to prison, as a matter of course, and the authorities would be satisfied that justice had been served. For their part, the young *mafiya* soldiers would willingly accept incarceration, because there was no better way to make one's bones in the world of organized crime, than to serve a prison sentence for killing someone. They would do their time and emerge wearing an intaglio of tattoos as a badge of honor, and no one would ever imagine that the crime had had nothing at all to do with drugs or the Russian mob.

Sokoloff was quite pleased with the plan, mostly because he felt it was the best way to get back to his idyllic retirement with only the barest minimum of exposure. With ten million dollars added to his nest egg, he might even be able to do a better job of avoiding future compulsory offers of employment.

It was only now, as he cradled the rifle and peered through the scope, that he remembered the thrill he had once gotten from taking another man's life.

Don't get used to it, Ivan.

The door opened and two men emerged from the clinic building.

Then again, he thought, *there's no reason not to enjoy it a little.*

He pulled the trigger.

3.

The call had come only a few minutes after Pierce had gone upstairs to visit his brother.

King—known to a dwindling few by his given name, Jack Sigler—didn't need to look at the caller ID; all the calls he received on this phone came from the same place. He answered without hesitation.

"It's Lew, King. Blue's...ah, otherwise occupied, so it looks like I'm on point for the moment."

Lewis Aleman was the resident all-purpose tech guy for Chess Team, the ultra-secret, off-the-books covert ops team of which King was the field leader. King wasn't sure if he was more surprised by the fact that Aleman had stepped up into a more administrative role or by the circumstances that had necessitated it. The last time the man known by the callsign "Deep Blue" had been "otherwise occupied," the possibility of human extinction—due to the spread of the lethal Brugada contagion—had been in the balance. Deep Blue, otherwise known as Tom Duncan—the former President of the United States—was the brains, eyes and ears of Chess Team. As the Chief Executive, he had created and nurtured Chess Team as a highly mobile, highly capable Delta unit, and when circumstances had forced him to relinquish his position as the leader of the free world, he had made running the team, now completely independent of the Department of Defense, his full time job. It did not bode well that he was out of the office.

King took that news in stride. If Deep Blue's absence was part of some new unfolding crisis, he would deal with it; that was what he did.

"Sorry to intrude on your vacation," Aleman continued, "but this one can't wait."

King almost laughed. He hardly thought of his extended-weekend fishing getaway with George Pierce as a vacation. But with King's girlfriend Sara Fogg working to establish a new HIV treatment protocol in Africa, and his adopted daughter Fiona staying with a new friend for the weekend, King had almost no reason to take personal time. If not for George's unexpected visit on short-notice, he would have been talking to Aleman in person…and he would have a better grasp on why Deep Blue was absent.

"Not a problem, Ale. Spill it."

"Yesterday afternoon, there was an incident near Phoenix. The official report is that a highway accident led to the release of an unspecified chemical contaminant. They've shut down a ten-mile long section of US Highway 60, just west of a little copper mining town called Miami, and established an exclusion zone. Nothing gets in or out."

"When you say 'they' you mean…?"

"The army. And while I grant you it's a little hinky that the military is running the show, that's not why I called."

"I take it the official story isn't the real story."

"That's what you need to find out." Aleman took a deep breath as if gathering his thoughts. "At 1435 local time—roughly thirty minutes after the accident—a video was uploaded to YouTube from the crash site. It took about fifteen minutes to go viral, but then…whoosh…it was gone."

"Gone?"

"Someone erased it completely from existence. Or at least they tried very hard to. A targeted borer worm virus hit the worldwide web and hunted down every permutation of the original. And I mean every single one, everywhere in the world, even still pictures taken from screen grabs."

"Is that even possible?"

"Believe me, it is, but to do it, you need some serious mojo—NSA mojo."

The capabilities of modern computer systems were not King's bread and butter, but what Aleman described sounded like the ranting of a conspiracy nut. For years, paranoid rumors of the government's, and specifically the National Security Agency's, ability to seize control of the flow of information on the Internet had spread like wildfire. King had always been skeptical; trying to control lines of communication was like trying to catch the wind in a bottle, and when you tried to do it, it almost always came back to bite you in the ass. Still, he trusted that Aleman knew what he was talking about. "So what's so important about this video?"

"I'm sending it to you now."

"How did you manage to get your hands on it?"

"I constantly monitor the Web for anything unusual, and this one certainly qualified. Normally, I would have dismissed it; it looks like something lifted from a horror movie. But when the virus hit the firewall, I decided to take a second look. Knowing where it came from, and how badly someone wants to keep it under wraps, I think it's worth checking out."

King's phone chirped as the file arrived and he held the phone away to watch the clip. For all the buildup, he was a little disappointed. As Aleman had indicated, it played like something from a low-budget experimental horror movie. He held the phone back to his ear. "It looks like Blair Witch Meets Bigfoot."

"Yeah, the monster kooks are all over this. The original video was probably only seen by a few thousand people, most of whom didn't take it seriously, but now ten times as many people are talking about the fact that the video is missing; they're sure someone is trying to cover up definitive proof of the existence of Bigfoot."

King pondered this. The video camera had captured only a brief glimpse of what appeared to be a hairy figure pounding its fists against the outside of a car window, but the image was blurred by movement. A moment later, the camera had presumably been dropped, and it thereafter recorded only sounds—human screams and bestial growls.

Because the video had come to him from Lewis Aleman, and because it was evident that someone had worked very hard to eradicate all trace of its existence, King had no doubt about its authenticity. He also knew why Aleman had brought it to his attention. "You think this might be Ridley's handiwork?"

Richard Ridley was the founder of Manifold Genetics—officially defunct, but still very much active—and monsters were his stock in trade. In their first encounter with Manifold, Chess Team had squared off against the Lernian Hydra, an almost unkillable beast thought to exist only in Greek mythology. More recently, Ridley, had learned the secret of animating *golem*, granted life to inanimate creations of stone, clay, crystal and bone, and unleashed them on the world, killing thousands. Chess Team was still smarting from their bittersweet victory against the madman; Rook was still MIA after carrying out his assignment against a target in Siberia, though Queen was now hunting for clues for his whereabouts…or the man's gravesite.

Stopping Ridley had become Chess Team's primary objective. Unfortunately, it wasn't their only mission. Recently, King had learned of a mysterious new threat with global influence, something they knew only as 'Brainstorm.' Aleman's workload had doubled almost overnight as he took on the task of trying to find loose threads in the Brainstorm network, thus far to no avail.

"Serious mojo," King muttered. Brainstorm had that kind of mojo. "Is there anything about this incident that definitively points to Ridley?"

"One thing," Aleman said, a hint of excitement in his voice. "It's hard to pick it out in the video, but if you freeze it at exactly the right moment, it's clear as day."

King's phone chirped again and he looked at the image file Aleman had just sent him. His eyes were immediately drawn to the object hanging from a leather thong around the creature's neck, and he realized that it was a good thing that George Pierce was already there.

4.

As they stepped through the doors of the rehab facility, King scanned the street for a passing taxicab.

"So," Pierce said, matching his friend's pace as they descended the concrete steps of the brownstone. "What can you tell me?"

King barely heard him. There weren't any taxis, but he had spied four men sitting in a black tricked-out Mercedes directly across the street, and now alarm bells were sounding in his head. He could only make out the facial features of the two sitting on the left side—they were Caucasian, with high Slavic cheekbones that made him think *Russians*—but it was the barely glimpsed object one of the men fidgeted with that commanded his attention.

Gun!

New York wasn't Fallujah or Kandahar. It wasn't even the same city it had been thirty years previously, in the grip of a war between criminal empires violently vying for dominance in the burgeoning crack cocaine trade. But no matter where in the world he was, King knew that a man sitting in an idle car, nervously playing with a gun, was a precursor to trouble.

Whether or not it directly involved him, whether or not he was their target, he knew immediate action was called for.

His instincts took over. He spun toward Pierce and tackled his uncomprehending friend into the rose shrubs on the side of the stairs.

There was a resounding crack as something struck the side of the building, knocking a chip of stone loose. Half a second later, the sound of a distant shot reached King's ears. The report had not come from the car; somewhere nearby, a sniper had just taken a shot, and only King's dumb luck in spotting the potential ambush had saved him.

I am the target, he thought. *Or George. Or both of us.*

That was all the thinking he had time for. The vegetation offered no protection and hardly any concealment from the unseen shooter, and now the men in the Mercedes were entering the fray. Three of the four doors, every one except the driver's, flew open to disgorge the passengers, all of whom carried old Soviet-era *Škorpion vz.* 61 submachine pistols.

"George, back inside! Stay low!"

He hauled the archaeologist to his feet and propelled him toward the staircase. It seemed unlikely that they would be able to survive the short crossing, but slim chances were better than none. Pierce stumbled against the steps and almost went down on his face, but King maintained a constant grip on his friend's biceps, and turned what would otherwise have been a face-plant into forward momentum. King managed to be a step ahead of Pierce, and wrenched the nearest door open, flinging it aside with such force that the hydraulic closer mechanism snapped off its mounts.

Gunfire erupted behind them and a storm of 7.65 millimeter rounds sizzled through the air above their heads. There was a noise like a jackhammer as some of the rounds smacked the other door; the rest of the burst shattered the ceiling plaster in the entryway. White dust rained down on them as King angled toward the lobby, still dragging Pierce, who was still struggling to find his footing. None of the bullets had found King, and he didn't think Pierce had been hit either, but there wasn't even a moment to stop and check.

On an impulse, he snatched up a pressboard side table, scattering dog-eared and tattered back-issues of *Time* and *People*, and heaved it toward the entry just as the first of the gunmen ventured through. The table struck the man in the chest and bowled him backwards into his companions.

King did not linger to survey the results of his hasty counter-attack. With Pierce now solidly on his feet it was time to go, but the only other way out of the lobby was through the electronically secured door to the left of the receptionist's window, and the gatekeeper had evidently fled as soon as the bullets had started flying. King analyzed the situation with the efficiency of a chess master, and immediately saw that getting through the door would require a lot more time than they had.

"Shortcut!" he yelled, diving headfirst over the counter and into the receptionist's office. He tucked and rolled, making the maneuver actually look easy; he'd done similar things in both training and actual combat, and it was a whole lot easier without fifty pounds of body armor, weapons, and other sundry pieces of gear hanging off his body. Still, all things considered, he would much rather have been fully equipped, because then he'd have something more than furniture to throw at the gunmen.

Pierce came over the counter a second later, his landing not quite as graceful as King's, and together they dashed into the hallway, seeking the building's emergency exit. Another staccato report hammered their senses as one of the attack squad unloaded a full magazine into the door's latch plate.

For just a moment, King considered turning the tables on the attackers. It was plainly evident that they weren't professionals. Even though he was unarmed, he felt certain of his ability to use the environment—in this case, the corridors and stairwells of the clinic—to isolate and overpower the men. If not for Pierce's presence, that was almost certainly what he would have done. But he couldn't take that chance with his friend…his brother.

He fixated on the overhead "EXIT" sign, and hastened toward it. Sometimes, as bitter a pill as it was to swallow, running away was the best option.

5.

Sokoloff spat a curse in his mother tongue as he saw his carefully laid plans disintegrate. Something had spooked the target; the damned impetuous junior Russian mobsters, so eager to spill blood, had probably jumped the gun. They might yet redeem themselves, charging into the brownstone with guns blazing like characters in a bad Hong Kong action movie, but it seemed equally likely that they would prove no more effective as the tip of the spear than they had as a diversion. With ten million dollars resting in the balance, to say nothing of his freedom, he had to see the target's dead body with his own eyes, even if meant risking exposure.

The black Mercedes peeled out noisily, and raced down the street, turning at the corner, presumably to block the alley that backed the line of brownstones. *At least one of them has a little sense*, Sokoloff thought.

He left the rifle where it was, confident that its eventual discovery would never lead the police to him, and he sprinted for the stairs leading down from the roof.

6.

An alarm started shrieking as soon as King hit the panic bar on the emergency exit. There would be little question now as to where they were, but it couldn't be helped. He burst through the door and with Pierce right behind him, raced into the alley.

He was immediately confronted with a choice: left or right?

Easy; right. The alley exited onto a cross street at either end, but the intersection to the right was closer.

He took off at a full sprint, and Pierce was right behind him. King was grateful that his friend seemed to grasp the urgency of the situation. The two of them had been in a couple of tight spots, and Pierce knew better than distract King with a lot of questions. Survival under the circumstances required quick decisions and instantaneous action; a single moment lost second-guessing one of those decisions, or worse, trying to explain them, might be the difference between life and death. That, and luck.

And sometimes, luck was just plain bad.

The black Mercedes cut across the end of the alley, screeching to a stop in a haze of rubber smoke. In his peripheral vision, King glimpsed Pierce's stride faltering, and he almost did the same as, twenty feet ahead of him, the car door flew open and the driver half-emerged, reaching over the doorframe with his Škorpion pistol.

"Screw this," King muttered.

As the muzzle of the submachine gun swung toward him, King lowered his shoulder and poured on the speed. Before the gunman could get off a round, King slammed into the door like it was a tackle dummy. The door crunched against the driver's upper chest, driving the wind from his lungs. The man's finger tightened on the Škorpion's trigger and lead began to spray randomly down the alley. King slid a hand along the outer surface of the window and struck the man's outstretched gun arm with the flat of his hand, deflecting it straight up into the air so that the last few rounds flew harmlessly skyward.

He rammed the door again. There was a satisfying crack as ribs broke under the assault and a spray of bloody spittle flew from the man's lips. King threw the door open, ready to meet whatever counter-attack might follow, but the driver simply slumped to the ground.

Pierce had sought refuge behind some trashcans, but King hastily waved him over. "George. Let's go. Our ride's here."

As if to underscore the urgency of the situation, the other three gunmen burst out into the alley, and immediately upon recognizing that King had taken down one of their number, opened fire.

The distance between the end of the alley and the rear exit of the clinic was just about the effective range of the short barreled Škorpions, but what they lacked in accuracy, they could make up for in volume. King didn't bother with further exhortations to his friend, but instead slid behind the wheel of the idling Mercedes and shifted it into drive.

He stayed low, barely peeking above the steering wheel, which he turned in the direction of the gunmen, while nudging the accelerator. The car swung around into the narrow space, and he immediately heard the harsh cracking sound of rounds perforating the windshield and whizzing through the space over his head to repeat the process on the rear window.

He angled closer to Pierce, giving him enough cover to reach the rear passenger-side door, but as soon as the archaeologist dived headlong into the rear seating area, King punched the accelerator and drove straight at the gunmen.

The fusillade diminished to nothing, either because the men had fled in the face of the onrushing Mercedes, or simply because they had simultaneously burned through their curved, twenty-round magazines and were all pausing to reload. King thought it the course of wisdom to leave that little mystery unsolved, and he kept steady pressure on the accelerator until the car broke out onto the cross street. Only then did he raise his head up to see where they were going, and once he did, he stomped the pedal all the way to the floor.

7.

Sokoloff exploded from the front door of the building just in time to see the black Mercedes skid around the corner. It wasn't too hard to divine the truth of what had happened. The target had somehow overpowered the team of gunmen and taken control of their vehicle. Sokoloff didn't care whether the junior mobsters were dead or alive, they had botched the mission and as far as he was concerned, they were as good as dead anyway. His entire focus was on the target.

He dashed down the block and rounded the corner to where his own rental car was waiting. He considered trying to somehow give chase, but that window of opportunity had long since closed. Literal pursuit would be an exercise in futility, but there were other ways to hunt a man.

He dug out his secure phone and hastily tapped out a message giving his employer the bad news. He didn't try to sugar coat it; as the American's were fond of saying, shit happened. The only way to save this, to save his ten million dollar paycheck, was to deal with the reality of the situation head on.

The reply came within seconds.

Your plan had only a 48.1% chance of success. You underestimated King's professional abilities.

Sokoloff made a rude comment about his employer's relationship with his mother, but the words that left his mouth did not reach his fingers. He simply waited for more information.

Standby. Reacquisition of the target is underway.

Sokoloff knew that his employer had vast resources at his disposal—the ability to access computer networks, traffic cameras and phone records. It wasn't too hard to imagine the mysterious figure sifting through a flood of digital information, looking for King's face, scanning cellular phone transmissions that might give away the target's location. He knew that his employer had been unable to hack King's communication network, but every cell phone call in the world still relied on the same basic technology—radio signals that were picked up and retransmitted through a vast electronic web. Somewhere, maybe only a few blocks away, King was probably calling for help, and even though the call itself might be wrapped in a blanket of security encryption, the simple fact of its existence would raise a red flag.

In the distance, he heard the sound of sirens and knew that it was time to move. As he pulled away from the curb, he mentally discarded the disastrous results of the attempted hit in much the same way that he had left behind the rifle. His employer had been correct; he had underestimated King, and he wouldn't make that mistake again. But a failure did not in any way subtract from his own considerable skill. He had been hunting and killing men long before the digital age, and he had succeeded in that profession, not just because of his ruthless efficiency, but also because he knew how to outthink his prey.

So, where will you go next, Jack Sigler?

8.

King pulled the shot up Mercedes into another alley only a few blocks from the site of the failed ambush, then looked back at Pierce. "You in one piece?"

The archaeologist, still lying prone on the back seat, took a deep breath, then with a grin commenced patting himself down as if checking for damage. "No worse for wear. So what the hell was that all about?"

King shook his head. "That's what I'm going to find out."

As they hiked out of the alley, King called Aleman. "Sorry to give you one more thing to worry about," he said, "but we just got hit."

He told Chess Team's tech expert everything he could about the ambush, which wasn't much, and answered the other man's questions as briefly as he could, with a minimum of speculation. That wasn't to say he didn't have a few ideas; the problem was, he had too many. He was fairly certain that the gunmen had been Russians—ethnically, if not nationally—and that represented a host of possibilities.

Chess Team had recently been involved in several operations in Eastern Europe: Queen was currently in the Ukraine. Rook had gone missing while on a covert mission to Siberia.

Further back, but by no means a distant memory, the team had taken out a terrorist camp on Russian soil—a technically illegal military action that could have been construed as an act of war, even though the terrorists would probably have carried out attacks on Russian civilian targets. And then there was the elephant in the room; King had just recently learned that his own parents were deep cover Soviet-era sleeper agents, willing to sacrifice their only son to accomplish their long range mission.

That was assuming, of course, that he, and not Pierce, had been the target, which actually seemed like an even more likely scenario, given that the attempt had occurred at the facility where Micah Pierce was currently residing. George Pierce was not without his own enemies; his archaeological investigations had more than once put him in the crosshairs.

King didn't tell Aleman any of this. Unsubstantiated musings would only serve to obscure the truth; the facts, sparse though they were, were all that mattered.

Aleman let out a low whistle. "I'll do what I can. Do you want to come in?"

King glanced at Pierce and considered the offer. It seemed extremely unlikely that the attempt was tied to the incident in Arizona, but he couldn't rule it out. As far as he was concerned, George Pierce was his brother—his only remaining link to a life that had been all but deconstructed by tragedy and betrayal—and the last thing he wanted was to put his brother in harm's way.

But George wasn't fragile or helpless. More importantly, his unique knowledge base might be just the thing to solve the riddle of what had happened in Arizona, and if Manifold was involved in that event, then the clock was already ticking. "No. We're going to Phoenix. Get us on a flight—George and me—soonest possible. We're heading to La Guardia now."

"Consider it done."

When King ended the call, Pierce asked: "Phoenix?"

"Yeah. Sorry, it looks like we're going on a different kind of fishing trip."

"If you're talking about Arizona, and not the mythological bird which is reborn from the ashes of its own immolation, I'm not sure how I can help. The American Southwest is a little outside my area of expertise."

King opened the file of the still photo Aleman had earlier sent and handed over the phone. Pierce studied the picture for a moment, then stared gravely at his friend. "So it's true. The Wookies are massing for an invasion."

King didn't laugh. "The medallion, George."

Pierce looked again, and this time his reaction was sincere. "Oh, that *is* interesting."

9.

"It's a silver *tetradrachm* coin," Pierce told King as they finally settled into their seats on an American Airlines 737 bound for Denver, where they would catch their connecting flight, "It's hard to make out with the screen resolution, but that's the likeness of Athena stamped onto it. As the namesake goddess of Athens, she was arguably the most important deity of the era—the embodiment of wisdom and intelligence, but also military strategy. The reverse side probably has the image of an owl, another symbol of Athena."

"Is it rare?"

"Today? Well, you aren't likely to find it in under your sofa cushion, but there are quite a few surviving examples. It was the most commonly used coin in the world going back to the sixth century BCE, and right up to the time of the Romans. With the spread of Hellenistic culture under Alexander the Great, the coins were used as currency as far away as India. They show up pretty frequently at digs, particularly at burial sites."

"Burials? I didn't think the Greeks followed the Egyptian custom of burying their wealth along with the body."

"They didn't. But it was a common practice to place a coin in the mouth of a dead person as an *obol*. A payment to Charon, to bear the soul of the departed to the afterlife."

"Pennies for the ferryman," King murmured. "So how did this coin end up in Arizona?"

"As a fashion accessory for a Wookie, no less," Pierce added.

"It's not a Wookie, George."

"Then what the hell is it?"

King shrugged.

Pierce pondered the problem a moment. "Okay, let's look at this objectively. That picture shows what appears to be some kind of bipedal animal. At first I thought it looked similar to Red." While Pierce wasn't part of the mission to Vietnam that took the team up against a pack of devolved Neanderthal women, he'd been told the story, shown pictures and knew exactly who Red was; Rook wouldn't let them forget. "But the more I look at the image, the more the hair doesn't make sense. There are different lengths. Different colors. It doesn't look natural. But it's definitely some kind of hominid. It's also wearing that coin as a medallion, like an amulet, and that most certainly is not typical primate behavior."

"So, maybe someone else…a human…put that thing around its neck. Like dog tags?"

"Possibly, though why they would choose an ancient Greek coin is beyond me. I think it's more plausible that the animal is exhibiting a higher degree of intelligence than its appearance suggests. It could be a living example of the fabled 'missing link' in the fossil record. Of course, that still doesn't explain the coin." Suddenly, Pierce's eyes grew wide as the pieces of the puzzle clicked into place. "You think this is something like the hydra, don't you?"

"We know for a fact that Hercules—Alexander—traveled to South America in ancient times. What I want to know, and I'm asking you in your professional capacity, is if you can give me a better explanation for how that coin wound up in Phoenix, Arizona?"

"Don't bullshit me, Jack. It's a lot more than that. You think that coin might be evidence that Ridley has found another monster from Greek mythology."

King heard the anxiety in his friend's voice when he spoke of Ridley. Only a couple years previously, Manifold Genetics' experiments with the remains of the hydra—a creature with the ability to instantly heal from any wound, and which unfortunately had not been simply the stuff of fairy tales—had resulted in Pierce being taken prisoner by Ridley, and subsequently used as a guinea pig in unspeakable medical experiments. Pierce had made a full physical recovery from the ordeal; whether he had recovered from the psychological trauma was another matter entirely.

King wondered if he hadn't made a grave mistake in dragging his old friend along on this outing. "George, right now I know as much as you do. Yeah, it could be Ridley. Or it could be something completely unrelated. That coin is our only clue, and that's why I immediately thought of you. But if you have even a hint of a bad feeling about this, we'll call the game."

"I may not be in your league," Pierce said, trying to sound confident, "but I know how to duck and cover when the bullets start flying. If this turns out to be a chance to take down some still functioning project of Ridley's, then I definitely want in. And if not…well, then the explanation for that coin's presence in the Americas might rewrite the history books. Just one thing, though."

"Name it."

Pierce grinned. "I'll be damned if I'm gonna let you call me 'pawn.'"

10.

East of Phoenix, Arizona — 0520 UTC (10:20 pm Local)

Nina Raglan stepped out of the cool, air-conditioned environment of the Toyota Land Cruiser and embraced the warm desert night. The temperature was still in the high eighties, but cooling as the rocky soil radiated its stored energy away into the cloudless sky. A life-long resident of the southwest, she thought of this as comfortable weather; in just a few short weeks, the daily low temperature would be closer to one hundred degrees Fahrenheit, and the highs would regularly exceed one-hundred and ten.

She was parked at the Campaign Trailhead, in the northeast part of the Superstition Wilderness. The Land Cruiser had nimbly negotiated the eight-mile long stretch of unimproved Forest Service roads connecting to state route 88, but from here, she would have to proceed on foot to reach her goal.

She circled the parked SUV and opened the rear hatch to reveal her gear, all carefully laid out in the storage area. She shrugged into her 1.6-liter CamelBak hydration pack, taking a perfunctory sip of tepid water from the bite valve—a water supply was the single most important factor in surviving a night in the desert, even in mild conditions. She then picked up the handheld video-camera, clicking it on to verify that the batteries were fully charged. She switched it to low-light infrared mode, and the dark display screen came alive, revealing the darkened landscape in an eerie green glow. Satisfied, she turned the device off and stuffed it in one of the large pockets of her lightweight windbreaker. She performed a similar function test on the Garman GPS device, noting her location on the backlit liquid crystal display, and the distance to the waypoint she had earlier entered into the device: just over six miles in a straight line, though it was unlikely the terrain would let her travel the shortest possible route. To get where she wanted, she would have to follow a series of trails weaving along the flanks of the Pinal Mountains.

Nina had only one more piece of equipment to add, something she hoped she would never have to use. She glanced nervously at the other two four-wheel drive vehicles parked at the turnaround; their owners were nowhere to be seen and presumably already in a camp somewhere down one of the trails. Confident that she was alone, she picked up the Glock 27 9-millimeter pistol, inserted a fifteen-round magazine with a grip extender, and then actioned the slide to chamber a round. The pistol went into the nylon holster, already threaded onto her belt, partially concealed underneath the windbreaker.

She didn't much care for guns or their potential to destroy life, but it was patently foolish to hike in the desert without a gun. That was a lesson her father had taught her very early in life, one of many, and she held his wisdom in high esteem. He was the reason she was what she was.

And what she was, at least in a professional sense, was one of the foremost scholarly researchers of everything covered by the vaguely defined term 'paranormal phenomena.' There were a lot of people involved in paranormal research, owing in no small part to the proliferation of reality-television programming that featured enthusiasts armed with cameras, audio recording devices and sundry other equipment, hunting for ghosts, monsters, aliens and pretty much anything that seemingly defied rational explanation and titillated the imagination. It was the "scholarly" part that Nina felt set her apart from the crowd. To be sure, many of the professional celebrity-caliber researchers—she did not think of them as colleagues—gave the appearance of applying the scientific method to their investigations, but just enough to give it a veneer of legitimacy. Most of their "findings" were a hodge-podge of mutually contradictory bits of errant data, pieced together into a mosaic that hinted at still greater wonders to be revealed and kept the ratings up.

Nina had been labeled a skeptic by her detractors, and to the extent that any scientist worth her salt tries to put aside preconceptions and think objectively, she was. Her mind was open to all the possibilities, but she had thus far seen no compelling evidence to make her a believer. Like her father before her, she earned her living writing the facts about so-called paranormal phenomena, free of sensational speculation, often exposing frauds and charlatans in the process. It wasn't exactly lucrative; people didn't like having their illusions exposed. But her books sold marginally well, and because she was—as one producer had told her—telegenic, she was often invited to appear on cable television programs, ostensibly as a skeptical foil to the raving pseudoscientists. Tall and slender, with long black hair and a face that seemed to have taken the best of both her father's Irish and her mother's Native American genetic traits, she was, as too many of her fan letters often pointed out, an exotic beauty. If not for her intractable refusal to play to the crowd, she probably could have had her own show, but her integrity to scientific principles was non-negotiable.

Deep down however, she wanted nothing more than to discover that there really was more in heaven and earth than science had thus far revealed.

Nina didn't expect to make such a discovery tonight.

She closed the door on the Toyota, extinguishing the only source of artificial light, and she was plunged into the near total darkness of the desert night. After a few moments however, her eyes adjusted and she saw a wondrous landscape, painted in the faint silver of starlight. The craggy peaks of the Superstition Mountains stood in stark relief against the velvety night sky. There was a tiny LED squeeze light on her key-chain, and a much larger MagLite under the seat of the Land Cruiser, but she resisted the impulse to light her way by such means. She was, after all, trying to sneak into an area that had been designated by the authorities as an exclusion zone.

In the last twenty-four hours, the nationwide paranormal community had been set on fire by the strange reports coming out of Arizona. After filtering through the paranoid tangents and discarding probably erroneous exaggerations, Nina had been able to piece together the facts—if they could be called facts—that had triggered the current conflagration.

According to the most reliable sources, an unknown bipedal creature had caused the multi-vehicle accident that had temporarily shut down a section of Highway 60. On the national scene, it was being called 'Bigfoot' or '*sasquatch*,' a term derived from the Salish word for 'wild man,' which originally had applied only to the legendary ape-like creature that roamed the forests of the Pacific Northwest. Stories of a similar creature were to be found in almost every part of the world, from the Yeti, or Abominable Snowman, of the Himalayas, to the Skunk Ape of the Florida Everglades, and Arizona was no exception. According to locals, at least the few of them attuned to the chatter, the accident had been caused by the Mogollon Monster.

Nina had followed the Internet discussion forum threads back to the earliest posts, which contained links to a video that had evidently been removed. Later threads angrily decried the removal as censorship, but several of them focused on what had been on the video: a fierce hominid, or possibly a primate, attacking a young woman in a car, immediately following the highway accident.

Nina had grown up with stories of the Mogollon Monster. It was reputed to be a hominid, ranging from six to eight feet in height, covered almost entirely in long dark hair. Some people who claimed to have encountered it reported a strong smell, similar to the odor of a skunk, and said that the generally shy creature produced whistling and shrieking noises. The only remotely violent behavior associated with the creature was a tendency to throw rocks at campers from a distance. The idea that such a reportedly peaceful creature would attack a car seemed as unlikely as...well, as unlikely as its existence in the first place.

Cryptozoology had always represented a troubling subclass of paranormal research for Nina. It was ostensibly nothing more than a search for new animal species, and as such, firmly rooted in the principles of science. Cryptozoology didn't require you to weigh in on heavy philosophical subjects about what happened after death, or whether the possible existence of extraterrestrials was at odds with religious beliefs. There were even a few examples of cryptids—mostly animals thought to be long extinct—that had been verified.

But science cut both ways. For an animal species to avoid extinction, it had to play a functional role in its ecosystem—it had to eat to survive, and that kind of biological impact produced tell-tale evidence. Even more importantly, animal species required a minimum population size to avoid the negative effects of inbreeding. The existence of the ubiquitous lake monster, for example, seemed very unlikely because for the species to remain extant, there would have to be, at a minimum, a dozen or more breeding pairs at any given time. Decades of searching had not revealed a shred of evidence to verify the existence of a single monster swimming in the depths of Loch Ness, much less the remains of the thousands that must have lived and died over the course of several millennia. Such details however rarely seemed to bother the true believers.

Nina didn't think the Mogollon Monster was responsible for the events that had closed Highway 60, and she wasn't hiking across the Superstition Wilderness to find proof of the creature's existence. She expected to find only a very rational, banal explanation for the accident and the subsequent enforcement of the exclusion zone, and when she returned with proof, she would write about it. If she learned something else, something unexpected, she would write about that with the same objectivity. That was what she did.

Though barely discernible in the darkness, Nina had little trouble keeping to the trail, which followed a creek bed along the western slope of Pinto Peak. The course of both the creek and the trail—which according to the guidebooks, had been in use since prehistoric times, and in the not so distant past, had been used by the Apaches and by US Army soldiers hunting them—had been determined by nature; like the water that periodically flowed down Campaign Creek, the trail followed the path of least resistance, through the narrow divide between the craggy mountains.

Nina had lapsed into a natural rhythm, her legs no longer complaining about the constant climb. After about two hours, she crested the high point on the trail, still well below the level of the surrounding peaks, and began the somewhat trickier task of descending the other side in the darkness.

As she started down the path, she checked her GPS. She was more than halfway to her objective, and soon would turn east along Cuff Button Trail. If she kept this pace, she would be in position to observe activity in the exclusion zone well before dawn.

Her sense of satisfaction was short lived. As soon as she put the Garman back in her pocket, she realized that the few moments spent staring at the screen of the device had deprived her of her night vision. Even as she cursed her stupidity, an unseen loose rock shifted beneath her foot. She went down on her backside, sliding unceremoniously about ten feet down the trail. The coarse terrain scraped her legs through the rip-stop fabric of her pants, which nonetheless protected her from serious damage. The same could not be said for her bare hands; she had instinctively flung her arms out for balance, taking the impact of the fall on the heels of her hands, which were then nearly shredded by the short slide down the rocky trail.

She cursed her bad luck, instinctively cradling her scraped and bleeding palms. But even as the echoes of her oath and the sounds of tumbling rocks jarred loose by her fall were swallowed up by the night, she heard another noise that turned her blood to ice.

It was one of those sounds that everyone recognized instantly, even if their only experience with it was from movies and nature documentaries—a rapid clicking sound, almost like a party noise-maker.

It was the unmistakable buzz of a rattlesnake, and it was close. Despite her familiarity with the desert and its many diverse and potentially deadly denizens, Nina did what most people do when surprised by a venomous snake: she screamed.

11.

King and Pierce were only about a quarter of a mile away when a shrill scream broke the otherworldly quiet. The two men exchanged a brief glance and then, as if motivated by a single mind, turned and headed back up the trail at an urgent but prudent jog.

Faced with essentially the same problem—how to approach the exclusion zone surreptitiously to conduct a covert investigation—King and Pierce had arrived at the same solution as Nina Raglan. Using the highway was a non-starter; that route would be subject to the heaviest surveillance. But the maze of trails running across the Superstition Wilderness was not as likely to be watched, particularly at night. That, at least, was what King was counting on.

He had done extensive map reconnaissance during the flight, scanning overhead satellite imagery of the area, researching other environmental factors that might have significantly altered the conditions on the ground. He had also done a little shopping.

Their first stop after picking up the rental car at Phoenix Sky Harbor International Airport, was at a large sporting goods store in Tempe, where his purchases were waiting to be picked up. Equipped with the very best survival gear, and perhaps most importantly, two sets of ATN Viper night vision monoculars, King drove their rented SUV east, away from the setting sun, along state route 88 and the Campaign Trailhead, little suspecting that very soon they would have company on the trail.

King's night vision device soon revealed an attractive woman, her dark hair pulled back in a ponytail, staring fearfully at her surroundings. Her eyes, which glowed like green coals in the Viper's display, were darting back and forth, and he realized that she was straining to see in the darkness. Her head snapped up at the sound of their approaching footsteps.

"Who's there? Don't come in any closer. I'm practically sitting on a rattler, and he's pissed off."

King froze in place and immediately began scanning the area around the woman for some sign of the snake that was menacing her. Most of the ground on the hillside was bare, but there was a jumble of large rock flakes a few feet below where she sat, and a few yards away up the hillside, there was a waist high sagebrush, either of which might have concealed a lurking rattlesnake.

"Hold still," King said, unnecessarily. "My name's... Call me King. I'm going to approach very slowly and see if we can't shoo Mr. Slithery away with a minimum of drama."

King could see her searching the darkness to locate him and found it a little disconcerting. He was standing right in front of her and could see her plain as day, but from her perspective, he was a disembodied voice.

He cautiously extended the tip of his lightweight aluminum trekking pole—another of the purchases he'd made from the sporting goods store—and tapped the rock pile near her feet. There was a blur of motion as something darted from beneath the rocks and bumped the pole.

"There you are," King murmured. The snake, probably a diamondback rattler, was incredibly fast, and as the woman had so eloquently put it, very pissed off. It was a wonder that she hadn't been bitten. He continued probing the creature's hiding place, hoping that it would do what most wild animals did when confronted with a threat that could not be overcome with their natural defenses, and move away. The snake struck again, closing its mouth around the tip of the pole and this time, it refused to let go.

King carefully pulled the relentless animal away from the rocks and away from its original intended victim. "Okay, ma'am, I want you to move very slowly to your right."

He could see the naked apprehension on her face, but she nodded and did exactly as he had instructed, shifting sideways at an almost glacial pace, without making a noise louder than a whisper. When she was about three feet away from where she had been, King gave the pole a shake and the snake let go, squirming once more into its hidey-hole.

"Ok, ma'am. You're safe now. You can get up."

"Nina."

"Right." King grinned. In the military, everyone except enlisted personnel in uniform was either a "sir" or "ma'am," until you were told otherwise. It was a habit that sometimes persisted, even though he was now in the super-secret, autonomous Chess Team, where military traditions did not apply.

"Uh, Jack?" Pierce said, from just behind him. "We have a problem."

King turned and found his old friend staring back down the trail. He also saw the 'problem' of which Pierce had spoken. Two figures, wearing digital pattern camouflage, from the tops of their desert boots to the cloth covers on their Kevlar tactical helmets, stood a few yards away. Another similarly dressed figure was covering them from about a hundred yards up on the hillside. Each weapon was equipped with a PAC-4 infrared laser targeting emitter. The laser beams were invisible to the naked eye but bright as day in the ocular of a night vision device like the Viper or the much more advance PVS-7s that each of the newcomers wore. The lasers reached out from the carbines to show where the bullets would eventually go: right into King's and Pierce's hearts.

Soldiers. They'd been caught by an army patrol.

One of the pair from below took a step forward and gestured with his carbine. "Face down. Hands where I can see them."

"What's going on?" Nina asked, unable to make out anything more than silhouettes.

"Shut up," snarled the soldier. "You're all in a shitload of trouble. Do as I say, or you leave here in a body bag."

With a sigh, King sank to his knees and remembered that there was, after all, an exception to the military "sir or ma'am" rule; it didn't apply when dealing with prisoners.

12.

From almost a hundred yards away, Ivan Sokoloff watched King's capture play out through his own PVS-7 device. This time, he didn't give voice to his rage, but inwardly he was seething. He had stalked King and Pierce across the desert for hours now, eschewing the trail for a hard scrabble across the slopes of the mountain, just waiting for an opportunity to take the shot and fulfill the contract. When King had doubled back to help the woman—an unexpected player in the drama that Sokoloff had spotted early on—the hitman had thought that his chance had finally come.

Although the desert trek represented a physical manifestation of his relentless pursuit, it was only the culmination of several hours of activity that had begun just a few minutes after he had delivered news of his failure in New York to his employer. He had no sooner arrived back at his hotel room when another text message had arrived, informing him of King's next destination: Phoenix, Arizona.

His mysterious employer seemed to know everything about King's itinerary, and had already booked Sokoloff a seat on the same plane. There was a subtle hint of urgency about the communiqué. Sokoloff could tell that there was something in Arizona that his employer didn't want King discovering before his death. Unfortunately, the rigid enforcement of transportation safety rules made it impossible for him to get a weapon on the plane. The new body scanning technology now made it impossible to bring even a ceramic knife aboard a plane.

Not that Sokoloff would have made the attempt in so public a fashion. Even though he had sat only thirty feet away from the man whose death would net him more money than he could possibly ever spend, and even though he had walked right past the unsuspecting King on three different occasions during the course of the flight to Denver, and once more on the way to Phoenix, the thought of a quick strike—perhaps a knife-hand blow across the windpipe, or a rigid finger, stabbed through the man's eye and into his brain—had never been more than an idle daydream. The problem with not being able to transport any weapons meant that, before he could go after King upon arrival in Phoenix, he had to stop and get some new tools of his trade.

His employer had streamlined that process. "Arrangements have been made," he had been told in another of the maddening text messages. His employer seemed to know King's every move, and had supplied Sokoloff accordingly, with a set of desert camouflage fatigues, night vision optics, and most importantly, a used but serviceable, Smith & Wesson Model 4006 .40 caliber semi-automatic pistol and three 11 round magazines. All of this had been waiting for him in a Nissan Xterra that had been left at the parking garage of the airport.

For a couple hours thereafter, he had followed King's progress electronically. His employer had acquired the GPS tracking signature for King's rental vehicle, allowing the Russian to reacquire his target and obviating the need to maintain visual contact, which might have risked exposure. It also represented one more opportunity lost; he could have pulled alongside King on the open highway and casually shot him as he drove, but no…a better opportunity would come.

Yet as he had hiked across the desert, reminded with every arduous foot of forward progress that he had lived the soft life too long to be doing this again, he had been unable to get within pistol range. He needed to be close; if he missed with the first shot, there was no telling what might happen. And because King and Pierce had night vision as well, sneaking up on them was doubly difficult. The appearance of the woman, hiking along blissfully unaware of the deadly cat and mouse game, had added a further complication, but her fall and subsequent cry for help had finally given him the chance he'd been waiting for.

And then the soldiers had appeared out of nowhere.

As he ducked his head down to avoid detection, he realized that he should be counting his blessings. Had he been only a few seconds quicker, he would have given himself away to the patrol. But that was cold comfort. King was now in military custody, and Sokoloff didn't have the first clue how he was going to overcome that obstacle.

The soldiers didn't question their prisoners, but quickly searched them, stripped them of their gear, zip-tied their hands and then ordered them to march down the trail in the dark. Sokoloff then heard one of the uniformed men speak into his radio. "Devil 2-1, this is Devil 2, over."

Sokoloff couldn't make out the reply. Somehow, the electronic voice reproduced by the radio's speakers didn't have the same acoustic quality.

"2-1, come up and sweep the area with your team. Let's make sure there aren't any more surprises out here, over."

There was another scratch of static.

"Roger that. Meet you back at the FOB. Devil 2, out."

Sokoloff kept his face tight against the warm desert ground, but now he was smiling. Maybe there was a way after all.

13.

A High Mobility Multipurpose Wheeled Vehicle (HMMWV) more commonly known as a "Humvee" was waiting a short way down the trail. King noted that it was the M998 variant of the venerable military transport vehicle, configured almost like a pick-up truck with a soft canopy over the rear cargo area and wooden bench seats on either side. The three prisoners were bundled into the back of the truck—no simple feat with their hands bound, and two of the soldiers got in as well, keeping them covered at all times with their M4s. During the forced march, Nina had made a few indignant inquiries that had led to a threat of being gagged, and so all verbal communication had ceased. Nevertheless, as they were herded into the transport vehicle, illuminated by flashlights, King managed to give Pierce a confident nod that said: *Don't worry. I'll take care of this.*

Despite his reassuring demeanor, King was still mentally wrestling to come up with a solution that would not only get them free, but also advance his mission. The recent decision to sever Chess Team from military control had given the unit a great deal more freedom, but it also had its drawbacks. Where once, he might have been able to simply give the commanding officer in the field General Keasling's phone number, and then at his own discretion, co-opt whatever resources he needed, now he would have to be a little more creative.

The three captives spent the next half hour enduring a torturous ride, where every bump pitched them into the air and brought them down again painfully on the metal deck or, as was more often the case, on each other. Eventually, the ride smoothed out a little, signaling that they had turned onto a somewhat improved road, and the Humvee picked up speed until reaching its destination only a few minutes later. Bruised and battered, they emerged from the vehicle under the harsh glow of overhead Klieg lights, powered by portable generators, in front of a capacious olive drab GP medium tent. King noted other tents, a motor pool with several different Humvee variants and even a large satellite dish. He also glimpsed a triple thickness of concertina wire encircling the entire compound, before he was ushered into the tent.

They were kept at gunpoint in a corner of the brightly lit tent for several minutes before being confronted by an Army lieutenant colonel whose nametape said: "Magnuson." King noted the matching unit patches on either arm—the screaming eagle of the 101st Airborne Division—and the air assault jump wings and combat infantry badge on his chest.

Magnuson didn't bother to introduce himself, but instead made a show of studying their respective driver's licenses. King's license identified him as Scott Nicholson, one of the many thoroughly developed aliases that he now used exclusively, in lieu of his given name.

"You're quite a cosmopolitan bunch," Magnuson observed. "A local, a New Englander, and a world traveler...are you actually a US citizen, Mr. Pierce?"

Pierce was unfazed. "It's Dr. Pierce, actually."

King jumped in quickly. "We're all citizens, Colonel," he said in a confident voice. "We've got a right to move freely about the country, but I'm not sure the same is true for US military forces. I think you owe us all an explanation."

Magnuson gave a short, humorless chuckle. "So we're going to play games then? You were caught trying to sneak into a designated isolation area."

"Really? I didn't see any signs."

"Cute." Magnuson checked his watch, and King noted that his brow furrowed, as if he had just realized he was late for an appointment. "So what's your story? Let me guess: you're journalists, right? Here to discover the 'real story'? Guess what? There is no real story. You put yourselves and my men in unnecessary danger by trying to sneak into the exclusion zone. Fortunately for you, no one is interested in prosecuting you for trespassing, so you're all going to be loaded on that Humvee, and evacuated back to Phoenix. Immediately."

Nina seemed mostly relieved by the news, but something about Magnuson's sense of urgency prompted King to stall for time. "Colonel, this is completely unacceptable. You seized our equipment…that's several hundred dollars worth of stuff. And my rental car is back at the trailhead. How am I supposed to retrieve it? You can't just swoop down and pick us up like this is some kind of conspiracy movie. We've got rights, and you're trampling all over them."

Magnuson checked his watch again, then answered impatiently. "You'll be able to sort all that out with the public affairs officer once you get to Phoenix, but right now, you need to get in that Humvee."

"I'm not going anywhere tied up like a common criminal," King pressed. He caught Pierce trying to hide a smile, while Nina looked completely shocked by his behavior. The lieutenant colonel frowned, and then fidgeted nervously with his watch. King could tell that the officer wasn't used to anyone challenging him, and decided to keep pressing the man. "You owe us an apology for this treatment. And that man who accosted us out on the trail. I want an apology from him, too."

Magnuson seemed to be on the verge of acceding to the demand when the tent flap opened and a fully outfitted soldier, with captain's bars on the front of his body armor vest, rushed in. "Sir, something weird is happening out here."

King craned his head around to look through the opening. "Weird" didn't begin to describe it. The ground outside the tent was covered in a carpet of mist, but it was no ordinary fog. The thick cloud of vapor shimmered like silver foil, and every few seconds, it flashed with discharges of static electricity. The mist crept in through the open flap, and King noted that it was also starting to seep in around the edges of the tent.

Suddenly, the sound of gunfire and shouting, interspersed with a shrieking noise like something from hell itself, shattered the quiet.

King dropped all pretense of indignation and turned to Pierce. "Okay, I didn't expect that."

INTRUSION

14.

East of Phoenix, Arizona — 0907 UTC (2:07 am Local)

For just a few moments, the heavy canvas fabric of the tent seemed like an impenetrable barrier, holding chaos at bay. The illusion was tested when something big crashed into its side, sending a ripple through the taut material that set the upright poles rocking back and forth.

Magnuson turned to one of his subordinates. "Keep an eye on them," he said, pointing to the still handcuffed trio. The officer had drawn an M9 Beretta from a holster on his hip. Something told King the 9-millimeter rounds from the pistol wouldn't make much of a difference.

The side of the tent snapped again and this time the inward bulge was not turned back by the durable material. Tension ropes snapped, or the pegs hammered into the ground to which they were attached were ripped free, and suddenly the tent seemed to fold in half.

King saw what was about to happen and shouted a warning: "Get down!"

He dropped to his knees and then half-rolled, half-fell onto his shoulder. He saw Pierce and Nina doing more or less the same, and then the roof caved in. The heavy fabric pinned him in place like it was weighted with sandbags. A few glimmers of light crept under the folds as some of the soldiers caught in the collapse struggled to get free, but King remained still and shouted for the others to do the same. Over the din of shots and screams, and the rustle of the tent's destruction, King heard the noise of something heavy, like sledgehammer blows, pounding the ground with a very familiar rhythm.

Footsteps, King realized. *Someone running. Or something…something that weighs as much as an elephant. Make that a lot of somethings.*

The olive-drab shroud grew tight around him as the steps began falling directly on the collapsed tent. One of the footfalls came down right next to his head, sending out a tremor that rattled through his skull. If the thing stepped on him…stepped on any of them…it would break bones or do internal damage.

The heavy steps moved away, sparing King, but he didn't know the fate of the others. With deliberate slowness, he began worming his way toward where he thought Pierce was, hissing his friend's name in a stage whisper.

"King? I'm here." It was Nina. He kept squirming forward until he felt his shoulder bump against her.

"Is George with you?" It occurred to King that Pierce had never actually gotten around to introducing himself to the woman they had met on the trail, but she seemed like a quick study.

"No. I lost track of him."

"Are you all right?" King kept the disappointment from his tone.

"So far. This would be a lot easier if I could get my hands free."

"We'll do something about that soon." King oriented himself toward what he thought was the shortest route to freedom. "Follow me."

A few feet from where he encountered Nina, King glimpsed a sliver of light. He cautiously poked his head out and tried to get a look at the mayhem that had descended upon the camp.

The shimmering mist was everywhere, hugging the ground and obscuring his view, but through it, King could see shapes moving—a few soldiers still standing their ground and firing their carbines, but many more running, pursued by enormous humanoid silhouettes. The air was alive with noise: the harsh crack of M4s, the screams of men dying and other inhuman shrieks, and in the distance, a deep bass rumble of thunder.

A soldier had fallen only a few feet from where King now lay. The young man's body was bent unnaturally; his upper torso had been twisted completely around. The heavy body armor had afforded little protection from the raw physical strength of the unknown attackers. King felt a pang of sorrow that another brave American soldier had fallen, but there wasn't time for grief. He spied a familiar object on the dead man's belt and scooted in close enough to grasp the hilt of the KA-BAR knife and draw it from its sheath.

Working by feel alone, King slipped the razor sharp blade under the plastic zip-ties binding his hands and gave the knife a twist. The plastic parted with hardly any effort. With his hands freed, he rolled back toward the collapsed tent and cut Nina's bonds as well. Only then did he poke his head above the blanket of mist.

The camp was completely unrecognizable. All of the tents had been knocked down, as had the overhead Klieg lights and the satellite dish. A fire was raging in one corner of the compound, possibly from one of the overturned diesel-powered electrical generators. The mist emitted an eerie glow that gave little illumination, but off in the distance, brilliant tongues of lightning mixed with fast-moving orbs of ball lightning were stabbing down from the sky, revealing the scene in brief flashes, like a strobe light on a dance floor.

In the surreal light, King saw a few soldiers still standing, but there were many more of tall, shaggy creatures identical to the one in the video Aleman had sent him. They seemed to be everywhere.

King saw Nina gaping in amazement at the mayhem, and pulled her down into the relative concealment afforded by the mist. With the naked KA-BAR stashed under his belt, he checked the fallen soldier's carbine.

The bolt was locked back, the magazine empty. He checked the gear pouches attached to the man's body armor vest, and found two full replacements. One went in the magazine well, the other in a pocket. If the soldier's fate was any indication, the 5.56-millimeter rounds hadn't been very effective against the creatures, but it was better than nothing.

"Stay close to me," he told the wide-eyed Nina. "And keep your head down."

His thoughts returned to Pierce, but a glance at the collapsed tent showed no hint of bodies—moving or otherwise—underneath the canvas in the area where he had last seen the archaeologist. He resisted the urge to start tearing the heavy fabric apart with his bare hands; it would have been a futile effort, for Pierce was plainly gone. He had either escaped on his own or...

King shook his head, refusing to consider the alternative. *George is here, somewhere, and I will find him.*

But even as he made that silent promise, he realized that the search for his friend could no longer be his first priority. He had come to Arizona to learn the truth about the strange creatures that had attacked the day before, and now, even though he was right in the middle of a major incursion by the same species, he still knew nothing about them, or what had prompted this attack.

He recalled how Magnuson had repeatedly checked the time in the moments leading up to the assault. The officer had known that something was about to happen and had wanted to get the detainees out of the way before that deadline.

No, I'm missing something. If Magnuson had known an attack was imminent, he would have been better prepared.

A heavy thumping, reverberating through the ground beneath his feet, cut short his musings. Even through the mist, he could see the creature lumbering directly toward him, its red eyes fixed on him like targeting lasers.

King didn't hesitate. He stood fully erect, facing the charging creature in a slightly hunched over tactical stance, and with the carbine pressed against his shoulder, flipped the fire selector to burst. He pulled the trigger twice in rapid sequence, what range instructors called a controlled pair, though in burst mode, his double-pull let loose six bullets in less than a second. All six rounds hit their intended target; at about thirty meters and closing, it was hard to miss. The tiny bullets, each only a little bit bigger in diameter than a construction nail, perforated the creature's broad, bare forehead in a tight grouping, right above the bridge of its all-too-human nose. Still the creature thundered forward.

King triggered another burst, lower this time, into where the thing's heart should have been, then hurled himself to the side, covering Nina with one arm. There was a tremendous thud behind him as the mortally wounded beast crashed to the ground.

It was hard to say whether the first bullet had done the job...or only the last...or if it had taken nine rounds to vital areas to stop the charge. Either way, King knew that fighting the creatures wasn't a viable option, and as the charge had revealed, trying to hide and wait wasn't much better.

He pulled Nina to her feet. "Come on. We're getting out of here."

15.

When the tent started to collapse, Pierce, in a moment of desperation, had started rolling sideways toward the edge of the enclosure. He'd crawled around in enough tombs and caves to know that when the ceiling started caving in, you wanted to be as close to an exit as you could. When he stopped rolling, he discovered that he had somehow rolled all the way out, and now lay in the open, shrouded in the shimmering silver mist.

He struggled to a sitting position, and immediately regretted his hasty escape. For just a moment, he considered trying to crawl back into the collapsed tent, like a frightened child hiding under a blanket from nightmare monsters in the closet. The problem was, these monsters weren't figments of his imagination.

The camp was a scene of absolute chaos. Dozens of soldiers tried to fight the intruders, and while they surely outnumbered their foes, the creatures were everywhere. Pierce felt foolish for having been so dismissive of them when King had showed him the picture; these things sure as hell weren't Wookies. In fact, they weren't like anything he'd ever seen before.

Primatology, like archaeology was a discipline of anthropology, and while his professional career had taken him down a much different section of that field, he remembered enough of his introductory studies to recognize that these animals weren't behaving like any kind of ape species, or *any* other animal species for that matter. They seemed more like rioting hooligans, in the grip of mass hysteria, smashing everything in sight. The soldiers' bullets were almost certainly injuring them, but the collective madness of the creatures, to say nothing of their imposing physical size, enabled them to shrug off all but the most lethal of wounds. Worse still, the creatures seemed to be everywhere.

"Jack—"

He caught himself immediately as he locked stares with a pair of eyes, gazing at him from across the collapsed tent. The eyes were bright red—*reflective*, Pierce realized, *adapted for low light*. While the creature looked at him, and he at it, he managed to remain perfectly still—paralyzed with fear, or intentionally trying not to provoke it, he couldn't say—but when it tilted its head back and let out a banshee wail, Pierce had only one thought: *Run!*

He could hear the pounding of the creature's footsteps as it trampled across the canvas, but he didn't dare look back. The view ahead wasn't much better, but he angled toward a gap in the mayhem. Running with his hands cuffed behind his back was awkward enough, but he felt compelled to duck his head to reduce the chances of catching a stray bullet, if only a little. When he reached the perimeter of the camp, he at last spared a glance over his shoulder and saw no sign of pursuit. That did little to cheer him; it seemed just a matter of time before he was noticed again.

The triple-strand of razor wire coils had been smashed flat in several places along the perimeter. It looked like a bulldozer had run over the barricade, but there were strings of bloody flesh and tangles of oddly fine hair clinging to barbs, indicating the creatures of flesh and bone had wrought this devastation. *At least there aren't any more of them coming in*, Pierce thought.

The silver mist hid the ground beneath his feet, but revealed a good deal more about the setting. The military camp had been situated about five hundred yards from a rocky hillside, and in the foreground, there were several large boulders that appeared to have broken off and tumbled down over the eons of history. Pierce fixed his attention on one of the rocks that looked big enough to hide him. Tentatively at first, but then driven by a primal instinct to get as far away from the carnage as possible, the archaeologist picked his way through one of the gaps and ventured out across the mist-shrouded ground.

He was halfway to his goal, when the earth fell away beneath his feet and he plunged headlong into darkness.

16.

Nina gaped at the motionless form on the ground, not so much unable to believe what she was witnessing, as unable to decide which part of the surreal experience was most unbelievable. Investigating paranormal phenomena was a little like buying a lottery ticket; she had often imagined what it would feel like to actually find some kind of real proof, but deep down she had never really believed it would happen. And certainly not like this.

That's a Mogollon Monster, she thought. She felt the man—King, he'd called himself—tugging at her hand, urging her to flee, and realized that she was reaching out to it with her free hand, as if touching the corpse might make it more real. "You killed it?"

Even as the words came out, she regretted the tone. She hadn't meant to make it sound like an accusation, as if his act of self-preservation was some kind of crime against humanity.

"Yeah," he replied, evenly. "And there's not much chance of them showing up on the endangered species list."

When Nina's hand reached the creature's hair, it felt softer than she expected. In fact, up close, the hair looked strange. Like a carpet created from the skins of different animals. She took hold of the hair and gave a tug. She gasped as a sheet of hair slid away from the body. "Oh my god, it's clothing, not hair."

King quickly inspected her discovery. The shifted cloak of hair revealed the creature's true skin. It was maroon, like congealed blood and covered in what looked like large goose bumps. He ran his hand across the skin. The bumps were hard, but almost slick, like wax.

As Nina lifted the hair up, he got a better look at the backside and immediately knew where the skins had come from. "We need to get out of here," he said. "That's human hair."

Nina's eyes went wide as she dropped the hairy cloak. King yanked her up. "Move!"

Nina tore her eyes from the dead creature and let herself be led away from the collapsed tent and toward an area where several Humvees had been parked in an orderly row…'had' being the operative word. All but two of them had been overturned, ripped apart or otherwise demolished.

As if sensing that her ability to think rationally was severely impaired, Nina's savior guided her to the passenger side of one of the surviving vehicles and opened the door for her. Like an automaton, she climbed in and then just sat there, staring through the windshield at the surreal landscape beyond. Just beyond the carnage, not too many miles in the distance, spears of lightning kept stabbing down out of the sky. A few seconds later, King got in on the opposite side and started the engine.

"Better buckle up," he said, even as he shifted the truck into gear.

The Humvee lurched forward and picked up speed, swerving around only the largest obstacles that lay along the path to escape. Nina resisted the impulse to curl up on the seat with her hands over her eyes, and instead tried to lend whatever help she could to the effort by keeping an eye out for threats emerging from her side.

In a few seconds, the Humvee reached the edge of the camp and rolled like a juggernaut over the already crushed concertina wire barrier. The transition from mayhem to relative calm was striking. The shrieks of the creatures and the sounds of sporadic gunfire were drowned out by the throaty roar of the Humvee's diesel engine and the crunch of rocks beneath its heavy-duty tires. They might simply have been on a drive through the desert, if not for the eerie glimmering fog and the near constant flashes of lightning. The ride however, didn't last long. To Nina's dismay, when they had gone only a few hundred yards from the military camp, King cut a tight U-turn, and pulled the truck to a stop facing back the way they had come.

"What are you doing?" she said, her voice strident, on the verge of hysteria.

In the silver glow, she could see the grim determination in his eyes. "I left a friend back there."

"How are you going to help him? Those things are all over the place."

"Yeah? Well, those things are part of the reason I'm here in the first place, so it'll be like killing two birds with one stone." Then, inexplicably, he smiled and patted her on the arm. "I'm not going to let a little thing like an army of crazed Bigfoots stand in my way."

"Mogollon Monsters," she corrected, unthinkingly.

That stopped him. "Muggy…what?"

"Bigfoot is from the Northwest. Here in Arizona, our legendary cryptid is called the 'Mogollon Monster.'" She spelled the word, which didn't look at all like the way it was pronounced: *muggy-un*. "There are obvious similarities, which have led a lot of people in the crypto-community to believe that they're the same…" She trailed off, realizing even as she spoke how ridiculous she sounded. None of it was academic anymore. All her knowledge about the Mogollon Monster was based on a patchwork of native legends and unverifiable anecdotes; all of that had just gone out the window.

King's earlier urgency now seemed more subdued. "Well that explains a lot. You're a monster hunter, right? That's what you were doing out here in the desert?"

"I'm...no." Nina struggled to find an explanation that didn't make her out to be a kook. She flashed back to Magnuson's accusation. "I'm a journalist and I do write about...folklore. But I wasn't looking for the monster; I didn't think there was such a thing."

A tight smile lifted the corners of his mouth. "I wish you had been right about that."

Pieces clicked together in Nina's head. "Hang on. You said you were here because of them, too. What did you mean by that?"

King stared at her for a moment then his eyes drifted to something behind her. "That storm isn't moving. The lightning keeps coming down in the same place."

"Don't change the—" She dropped her protest as the impulse to turn and look proved overpowering. Sure enough, the constant flashes of electricity and falling ball lightning appeared to be striking in the same area. Stranger still, barely visible against the strobing flashes, the night sky was unobscured by storm clouds.

Then, as if the purpose of the storm had merely been nature's way of getting their attention, the frequency of the flashes began to diminish, and about a minute later, the lightning ceased altogether. As the last report of thunder echoed away into the darkness, Nina saw that the silvery mist was also dissipating rapidly. A few moments later, a blanket of darkness and quiet settled over them.

"Okay, that was a little weird," King said, breaking the silence. He switched on a flashlight, but kept it covered with one hand so that it only produced a soft glow, enough for them to see each other, without being seen by anyone nearby. "The lightning and that mist...are those things that are usually associated with this Muggy Monster?"

His avoidance of her earlier questions did not escape Nina's notice. King might have come looking for the creature, but he obviously knew nothing about it. "Yes and no. Lightning...well, we get a lot of that in the desert. But that mist...I've heard stories about that as well, although not in connection with the monster.

"There are all kinds of reports of strange phenomena occurring in the Superstitions—like that mist. A lot of people believe that there are magnetic vortices, caused by all the iron ore in the ground, and that the mountains amplify the earth's natural energy. Others claim there are inter-dimensional doorways here. There are reports of people levitating, being transported miles away in the blink of an eye, or just vanishing completely." She forced a laugh. "If you ask me, you have to be crazy to want to live in the desert, and crazy people are apt to see a lot of crazy things."

"You sound skeptical."

"I am. I mean, I was. Until..." Her attempt at evincing confidence fizzled. "What about you? You say that you were here because of the Mogollon Monster. What did you mean by that?"

"It doesn't matter. You should be safe here for now." He picked up a soldier's helmet, presumably something he had taken from the camp during their flight, and settled it on his head, lowering the attached night-vision device into place.

"It does matter," she protested. "You clearly don't know anything about the Mogollon Monster or the Superstitions. And if you think I'm just going to sit here while the answers I'm looking for are right out there, *you're* crazy."

He swiveled the night-vision monocular out the way and stared at her appraisingly. "I'll admit having someone who knows about this stuff would be helpful. But I can't guarantee your safety."

"I didn't ask for your guarantee. I came out here on my own, and if necessary, I'll finish this the same way."

He smiled. "I seem to recall something about a rattlesnake."

Before she could protest, he lowered the monocular again, and then switched off the flashlight, plunging her once more into darkness. As her eyes adjusted, she could make out his silhouette as he peered through the windshield, looking across the desert to the ruins of the army camp.

"They're gone," he said finally, but something about his tone caused Nina's heart to start racing again.

"The Mogollon Monsters?"

He shook his head in the darkness. "Everyone."

17.

The scrape of something against his heels startled Pierce into wakefulness; someone was dragging him. He reflexively struggled against the grip, his hands searching the darkness for his captor.

"Easy, pardner." The voice was low, intentionally hushed, but most assuredly human. "I'm tryin' to help."

Pierce felt himself lowered to the ground, then the hand shifted position to help him to his feet. "Who are you?"

"Keep it down." The voice was calm, delivered with a thick southern drawl that Pierce couldn't quite place. "I saw you take a tumble and thought you might need a hand. Good thing too, because those...well, whatever they are...they started coming down a few minutes later."

The words unlocked Pierce's short-term memory...the attack on the military camp...his flight out into the desert. He didn't remember the fall, but his body did. He could feel fresh abrasions on his cheek and forehead, and his body ached. As he probed his injuries, he realized that his hands were free. "You cut me loose," he said, remembering to whisper. "Thanks."

"Didn't make a lick of sense to keep you trussed up like that. Come on. I think I see a place where we can hole up and let them pass by."

Pierce strained to hear anything other than the crunch of their footsteps, but the air was as still as it was dark. He intuited that the man with him had to be one of the soldiers from the camp, navigating the tunnel with night vision goggles. Resignedly, Pierce allowed himself to be led forward into the wall of blackness.

"Here. Hunker down. They're right behind us." The man was insistent, but strangely calm, as if fleeing from hulking humanoid monsters was an everyday occurrence.

Pierce did as instructed, aware of his heart thudding in his chest. After a few seconds, he heard other sounds—grunts, labored breathing, the slap of skin against stone—and almost gagged as a rancid odor, like a heap of rotting skunk flesh, filled his nose. It was the distinctive smell of the creatures that had attacked the camp—he had smelled it earlier, though not as strongly—during the mayhem. The creatures were indeed close, and getting closer, and Pierce expected at any moment to feel large hands close over him.

Instead, it was his guide's hand that reached out from the darkness to tap his shoulder. "Here. Take a look."

Something hard, about the size and weight of a small camcorder, was pressed into his hands. He realized that it was a night-vision device like the one King had given him earlier in the night. A green glow showed him which end was the business end, and he quickly held it up to his right eye.

Looking through the objective lens of the night-vision monocular was like watching a movie on a tiny television screen. It was hard to believe that what he was seeing wasn't just footage from a monster movie, but was actually taking place just a few feet away. A line of the enormous hominids was moving past the niche in which they were concealed. More than a dozen passed by as Pierce watched, and every single one of them carried a body—either the camouflage-clad form of a soldier or one of their own species—all dead, he assumed. What was most surprising to Pierce was the complete absence of the ferocity he had witnessed during the attack. The creatures moved with a single-mindedness reminiscent of ants trekking relentlessly between their hive and a food source. He sucked in an involuntary breath as one of the beasts turned its shaggy head and glowing eyes to look at him as it passed, but the creature did not even break its stride.

It was only as the monster moved away that he realized he had seen something else.

In the chaos of the attack on the military camp, he had seen the creatures as nothing more than enormous shaggy animals, driven by mindless instinct. But as they paraded by, he saw evidence of more complex behavior—one of creatures reached back and with a quick tug, removed the hair from its body—*much* more complex.

Holy shit, Pierce thought, *the hair isn't natural.*

The photo he had seen earlier, had showed one of the creatures with a single ancient Greek coin, worn like a medallion on a string around its neck; it was the very aberration that had brought him here. And it was nothing alongside what he now beheld.

Coins, rings, bracelets…every manner of precious or semi-precious metal ornament adorned the creatures—every last one of them. The treasures were threaded like beads onto strings of what looked to Pierce like strands of twisted gut, and they were worn like amulets or totem necklaces. Some of the strings were heavy with dozens of pieces of jewelry; evidently, the creature whose image had been captured digitally was a pauper among his peers—*or hers*, Pierce thought.

For just a moment, the horror of the attack was eclipsed by this new mystery. This was a form of complex animal behavior…evolutionary behavior. Pierce didn't know exactly what the explanation was for all of it, but he knew that it almost certainly had nothing to do with Manifold Genetics.

After a few minutes, the procession ended; the last of the enormous creatures vanished down the adjacent tunnel.

It was only then that Pierce had an opportunity to scope out his surroundings. But for the fact that he had just witnessed at least a couple dozen of the creatures passing, he would not have believed that he was in a cave. The monochrome green of the night-vision device revealed only upright walls of dark rock in every direction.

"I'm gonna need that back soon, pardner."

Pierce turned to get his first look at the man who had evidently come to his aide. The man's digital camouflage uniform showed him to be a soldier. There was a patch with three chevrons affixed to his body armor vest, and next to it a name tape that read "De Bord." It was impossible to make out much detail in the green display, but Pierce thought the man looked quite a bit more mature than most of the enlisted soldiers he's seen in the camp. The sight of the uniform slammed a door on his musings about the extraordinary creatures, and reminded him that a lot of people had just died... King might have died.

But they just ignored us. We're obviously on their turf now; why didn't they attack?

It was a mystery that would have to wait. Darkness engulfed him as he lowered the monocular and extended it toward the soldier.

"Sergeant De Bord is it?"

There was a pause as the other man took the goggles from him. "That's right." De Bord sounded confused by Pierce's knowledge of his identity.

"I saw your name tag. So, am I your prisoner?"

De Bord chuckled. "I reckon we've got bigger things to worry about. For now, let's just focus on getting out of here, and finding your friend."

"I'm not too sure where 'here' is. What happened?"

"I saw you take a tumble into this here cave. Those…whatever they are…they were headed your way, so I went in after you."

Pierce felt a guiding hand on his shoulder and allowed the soldier to steer him out of the recess where they had hidden.

"We can't be more than a hundred meters from the opening," De Bord continued. "Just keep a hand on my shoulder and we'll be outside in no time flat."

"Do you have a flashlight? I don't think we have to worry about those creatures anymore."

"I hope you're right about that. Hang on."

Pierce winced as a light flared in the other man's hand, revealing the cave walls in their true color—dark rock of indeterminate composition. De Bord directed the beam down the passage in the same direction from which the creatures had come, and started walking with Pierce in tow.

As they moved along the cramped passage, Pierce decided to exploit the sergeant's evident willingness to engage in conversation. "So I take it the Army is here because of those creatures, right? What do you know about them?"

"Not a whole helluva lot. They came out of nowhere, wrecked everything, and then just like that, decided to skedaddle. The rest of it is all above my pay grade. I just do what the brass tells me to do." He stopped abruptly and directed the light overhead.

The circle of illumination on the rock ceiling showed nothing particularly remarkable, but in the ambient light, Pierce saw that the tunnel ahead sloped upward and ended abruptly.

"What is it?" he asked.

"I don't understand," the sergeant said, turning to face him. "This is where you fell in…where I found you. But there's no opening."

Pierce felt cold dread creep over him. "Maybe we passed it already."

"Not a chance." De Bord pointed to something on the floor—a broken loop of black plastic a few inches long. "I cut that off your hands right where I found you. The mouth of the tunnel was right here."

Pierce stared up again, but there wasn't even a hairline crack in the rocky expanse overhead. It was as if the earth had closed the door behind the retreating creatures, sealing them in.

18.

A closer inspection of the camp only confirmed what King had seen from a distance. There was abundant evidence of the battle—wrecked tents and equipment, discarded weapons, a littering of brass shell casings, and everywhere, spatters of blood slowly drying to a black crust in the warm desert air—but there was not a single body, human or otherwise, to be found. Hoping against hope, King tried calling Pierce's cell phone, but the call went directly to the archaeologist's voice mail.

Nina stayed close as they ventured cautiously into the perimeter, but stopped a few steps in and bent to illuminate the ground with a small flashlight. "Look at this."

King glanced quickly at her find, but did not immediately grasp its significance. "A footprint?"

"Look at it," she insisted. "It's huge. What do you wear, size 12? It's at least six inches longer than your foot."

He made no effort to hide his irritation. "We already knew they had feet. And that they're big."

"But it's hominid, for sure." She pointed to the round depression made by the heel and ball of the foot, then counted the toes as if doing so would emphasize her point. "This has toes. Humans are the only species on the planet with a foot like this."

"Not anymore." He stood and did a quick visual sweep of the area. "I don't see what the big deal is. I thought monster footprints were a dime a dozen."

She shook her head. "Most are provable fakes, and the rest are highly suspicious. This one...well, we know exactly what made it. It's real, tangible proof."

"Put this in practical terms for me. What are we dealing with here? Could these things be mutants of some kind?"

She shrugged. "The legends of the Mogollon Monster—and other creatures like it—go back to prehistoric times. I suppose in a scientific sense, they are the result of a mutation—that's what drives evolution—but it's more likely that they're a lower branch on the evolutionary tree. An ancestor species, or at the very least a distant cousin. We know that hominid species like this had to have existed in the past; this just proves that they're still around."

King shook his head. "I'm not interested in proving anything. I want to know where these things come from, and why they are on the warpath. In case you weren't paying attention, that wasn't a lone monster wandering the hills harassing hikers. That was a whole tribe, and I think if there'd been a tribe's worth of these things roaming these hills all this time, someone would have found proof that was a little more definitive."

"That's why it's so... Wait, what are you trying to say?"

"Think about it. Nothing like this has ever happened. The attack on the highway, this...what's different now?"

She blinked at him.

"The attack happened simultaneously with the appearance of that mist," he continued, not trying to make a point so much as review the disjointed facts for his own benefit. "Those soldiers were expecting it, or at least expecting something to happen."

"So you think this could be the result of something the government is doing?"

"You're the expert on this kind of thing. What do you think?

She laughed without much humor. "Being an expert on paranormal phenomena is a little like being an expert on Santa Claus. I can give you chapter and verse on the mythology and the reports, but no one is an expert on the real cause. That goes for paranoia about secret government conspiracies, too. You can't really be an expert on something that's completely imaginary."

"It's not all imaginary," King muttered. His experiences, both with government shenanigans and phenomena well outside the accepted scientific norm, probably made him more of an expert than she, but that wasn't something he was going to share with her. "The mist, those creatures…it's all connected somehow. We're not going to find our answers here."

"Where then?"

King stared at the footprint, one of dozens—perhaps hundreds—that were clearly visible leading both into and away from the camp. The creatures' path of egress was clearly marked, and it wouldn't take the skills of a legendary Indian scout to pick up their trail…a trail that would almost certainly lead him to George Pierce, or at the very least, resolve the question of his friend's fate. But his intuition told him that the answers to the important questions would not be found in the lair of the Mogollon Monsters. "Lightning isn't supposed to strike the same place twice, right? I'd say that's a good place to start."

19.

De Bord continued to sweep the dead end with his light, muttering in disbelief. "It was here. I know it was."

Pierce didn't know what to say. He had no recollection of his fall, but the evidence that this was where they had both entered the tunnel was right there on the ground. He knelt and picked up the discarded plastic tie. "Maybe we took a wrong turn. Maybe one of those creatures picked this up and dropped it here."

"There were no turns," De Bord insisted. "And I recognize this place."

"Then there's some other explanation. Whatever it is, we're not getting out this way."

De Bord appeared reluctant to accept that assessment, but after several more minutes of searching with both his eyes and his hands, he relented. They made their way back to the niche where they'd earlier hidden, and then kept going.

The tunnel gradually opened up, and before long they saw—and smelled—evidence of habitation. Pierce resisted a scientific curiosity to examine the piles of fresh scat that littered the floor; a glance was enough to tell him that the creatures were omnivores, but there was nothing of behavioral significance in the distribution. The creatures were not marking territory or defining their living space, but merely answering nature's call as they made their journey. Aside from the stench of their excrement, the air in the tunnel seemed to be fresh, and that was an encouraging sign.

Acting on a sudden inspiration, Pierce took out his phone and checked for a signal. There wasn't one, but as they progressed, he watched for bars to appear. If he could get reception, it might indicate the proximity of an opening to the surface. He was about to explain this idea to De Bord when the soldier abruptly raised a hand, and then pushed him back a few feet.

"There's a whole mess of those things up there," he whispered, dousing his flashlight.

Pierce felt his pulse quicken. "What are they doing?"

"I didn't take the time to look. Hang on, I'll check it out."

Pierce heard the soft rush of fabric scraping against the floor as De Bord crawled away, and then after a minute, heard it again indicating the soldier's return. "They're lining up the bodies." There was a hint of disgust in the man's tone. "Going through the pockets of the dead, it looks like."

Pierce withheld comment on the unusual behavior, but it was another significant clue. While robbing the dead might be a contemptible act for a group of humans, it wasn't something that mindless animals did; for a predator or a scavenger, a corpse was just so much meat. But these creatures evidently possessed the capacity to value objects, even those that had no utilitarian purpose.

"I want to see. Can you give me the night vision device?"

De Bord sighed wearily. "I guess there's nothing else to do right now, but be careful. If they see us, we're gonna be up shit creek."

Pierce wasn't so sure about that, but took the monocular from the soldier and held it to his eye as he crawled forward to the edge of the chamber where the creatures were engaging in their own peculiar funerary rites.

There were at least two dozen of the creatures moving about in the cavern, and about half that many lined up against a nearby wall unmoving, presumably dead. Pierce noted the care that had been taken in arranging their bodies; they were all oriented in the same direction, limbs straightened against the onset of rigor mortis, and arms crossed on their chest. Their totem necklaces had been removed but Pierce caught a glint of something metallic in the mouth of each fallen creature—an *obol*, he realized.

The human remains had not received such elaborate treatment. The bodies of the fallen soldiers, too many for Pierce to count, had been piled up in the center of the chamber where the creatures were meticulously searching each one in turn. Pierce saw watches and rings torn from hands, and coins shaken from wallets. The loot was laid out carefully in a pile, and when a body yielded nothing more, it was dragged to another mound on the wall opposite from where the fallen creatures lay. Amid the uniforms of dead soldiers, Pierce saw other human remains—some in an advanced state of decay, some withered away to mummified husks but still clad in tattered jeans and hiking boots.

They've been doing this for a while, he realized. He had read up on the history of the Superstition Mountains during the long plane ride; every year, going back at least a century, a few hikers, many of them dreamers searching for the Lost Dutchman gold mine or some other bit of treasure from folklore, vanished in the desert wilderness. Here, it seemed, was the answer to that mystery.

It didn't, however, explain the *tetradrachm*.

The creatures spent only a few more minutes searching the dead. When they had finished their grisly task, the collected items were gathered into what looked like a leather sack, carried by one of the creatures who already possessed a prodigious totem necklace. He barked stridently to the rest of the group, and then as if answering to a collective consciousness, they all fell in behind him and moved single file into another tunnel on the far side of the cavern.

Pierce knew that his only priority should have been finding a way out, but scientific discovery had always been his single motivating purpose. Teaching, lecturing and writing. Those were the things he had to do as a professional, but working in the field, uncovering mysteries so ancient that no one even knew they had been forgotten, was what drove him. He had wanted to be an archaeologist from the moment he had first watched Indiana Jones trekking through the jungles of Peru in the movie *Raiders of the Lost Ark*. Given a choice between escaping danger or making a spectacular discovery, Pierce had only one guiding principle: *What would Indy do?*

As the last of the creatures vanished into the passage, George Pierce moved forward into the burial chamber.

20.

After driving cautiously along an unpaved Forest Service road for about five miles, headlights off to avoid drawing attention to their presence, King spied a distant blaze of light in the objective of his PVS-7. He stopped the Humvee in the middle of the road and got out for a better look.

The source of the illumination was, even at a distance, easily recognizable as another military compound. The camp was at least twice as large as the forward operating base where they had been taken after being captured, and was situated only a few hundred yards from the long asphalt ribbon that had to be US Highway 60. The size and close proximity to the highway suggested that this was probably the central command for the military exclusion zone. It was only when he peered through a pair of binoculars he'd found in the Humvee that King realized that this camp had also been attacked.

This base had fared better than the FOB from which he and Nina had escaped. Teams of soldiers were busy working to repair the damage, most of which had occurred along the northern edge. Closer to the center of the camp, a row of Humvees was lining up in readiness to venture outside the wire.

King knew the patrol was probably going to find out why the other base hadn't reported in. It was time to get off the road.

Before he could return to the Humvee, he spied another vehicle approaching the camp from the east along a track that cut across the desert. With its blazing headlights, it was impossible to see the vehicle using night-vision, but King's suspicion that it was not a military truck was confirmed when it pulled up to the base. In the glare of the portable generator-powered sodium vapor lamps, and aided by the binoculars, King saw a white SUV with an indistinct logo painted on the door.

The occupant, a balding man in civilian clothes, got out and was met by a several soldiers who emerged from a central tent. Curious, in spite of the need to find concealment, King watched the brief but animated exchange between the civilian and the officer in charge. It ended when the civilian angrily got back in his vehicle and left in a cloud of dust.

King hastened back to the Humvee where Nina waited impatiently. "Well? Do you have your answers?"

King turned a switch and the Humvee's diesel engine rumbled to life. "No, but now I know who does."

21.

"What is that?"

Nina glanced over at King, but in the darkened interior of the Humvee she could only distinguish a vague silhouette. His hand was outstretched, pointing. "What is what?"

"Oh, sorry. There's a bunch of buildings. Some kind of mine operation?"

She nodded. "Must be the copper mine. It closed a couple months ago. Some big multinational bought them out and shut it down. Put a lot of people out of work. It was a profitable operation, but I guess the new owner thought they could make more by closing it down to drive up copper prices."

"I wonder if there isn't another explanation," King said, thoughtfully.

Nina wasn't sure what the economic hardships of a small mine had to do with the attacks by the Mogollon Monsters. It was evident that her new investigative partner saw a connection, but he had hardly said a word to her since leaving the road surreptitiously following the vehicle he had seen leaving the military camp. Nina hadn't actually seen the SUV; they had been driving without lights, and she had only caught a few glimpses of the other vehicle's tail lights in the distance.

"The mine looks completely shut down," King observed. "But it looks like our friend is going to a structure north of the processing facility. If I'm not mistaken, the lightning we saw came down near here."

Nina did her best to follow his reasoning. "You think maybe whatever they're doing has something to do with the attacks?"

He didn't answer her directly. "Do you know anything about the company that bought out the mine? A name?"

"No. I'm sure they mentioned it in the news reports, but it's been a several weeks."

"I'll see if I can't find out." A subtle glow illuminated King, the display of a cell phone that he pressed to his ear. "Call Aleman."

She listened impatiently to half of a conversation in which King asked Aleman—whoever that was—to look up information on the copper mine.

"Bluelight Technologies," she heard him say. "Any connection to Manifold? Right…Well, you keep digging on your end. I'm going to go in for a closer look… Roger that, King, out."

The glow vanished, returning Nina to near-total darkness as the Humvee continued along the uneven dirt road.

"You're military, too, aren't you?" Nina asked after a few minutes.

"What makes you say that?"

"The way you handled that gun during the attack. Your familiarity with this Hummer. And then there's the whole 'Roger that, King out,' thing just a second ago."

"I was in the army for a while." There was a hint of embarrassed humor in his tone. "Some things you never forget."

Nina sensed he wouldn't reveal anything more on that subject, so she tried a different tack. "What's Manifold?"

She saw the shift in his silhouette as he turned to look at her for a moment, then turned his eyes forward again. "Manifold is...or was, rather...a biotech company run by a guy named Richard Ridley."

"Biotech? So you're going with your theory that the creatures are mutants?"

"Right now, I don't have a theory. I'm just putting the coincidences together. Manifold is very bad news, and my job is to find them, root them out, and shut them down."

Nina knew better than to ask who had given him that job, but there were clues aplenty in the subtext. What was even more evident was his understated dedication to that mission. It was the kind of single-mindedness that drove a lot of the believers in paranormal phenomena—drove them, and sometimes blinded them to the obvious answers. And everything else that most normal people considered important.

Still, he didn't seem crazy.

"And Bluelight Technologies," she continued. "That's who owns the mine now?"

Before he could answer, a familiar humming noise signaled an incoming call on King's phone. Nina saw the glow of the display then to her surprise, heard King say: "Ale, you're on speaker. With me is Nina...Raglan, was it? She's a special consultant on local affairs."

There was a brief lag, and then a weary voice said: "I understand. Ms. Raglan, I'm Lewis Aleman."

"Umm...hi."

"So, Ale, what can you tell me about Bluelight Technologies?"

"Quite a lot, actually...and yet, at the same time, not much. It's a new firm, only a few months old. Founded by one Aaron Copeland. Copeland is a physicist, Masters from MIT. Worked at CERN for a while, then about a year ago, he dropped off the radar. When he popped up again, it was at the helm of Bluelight."

"Physicist," King repeated. "Narrow that down for me."

"He's published several articles on using phase states of matter as an alternate energy source. I can't really tell you what any of this stuff means, but it sounds like science-fiction. The real kind though, heavy on the science, and without laser gun battles and green-skinned babes. Bluelight's mission state-ment—and I'm quoting here— is 'pioneering alternative energy sources for the 21st century.'"

"There's no way a start-up would have the resources to shut down the mine operation," Nina observed.

There was a brief pause and Nina wondered if she had said the wrong thing. "That's a very astute observation," King said, without a trace of insincerity. "Bluelight has some significant financial muscle behind them. Ale, can you follow the money?"

"Easier said, King. They're not publically traded. I can tell you this though; right now, Bluelight has just one client."

"The government?" Nina said.

"Ah, a point to the lady. Specifically, Bluelight has a con-tract with DARPA."

Nina knew all about DARPA—the Defense Advanced Re-search Projects Agency—the military's R&D arm. The agency had become something of a bogeyman for paranormal enthu-siasts, particularly in the UFO community, who imagined DARPA scientists working feverishly in secret laboratories at Area 51, to reverse engineer alien technology from crashed spacecraft.

"'Who' isn't as important as 'what,'" King said. "Forget the money trail for now, Ale. See if you can figure out what Copeland is trying to do out here. Go through his published work again; there's got to be a thread we can pull on to unravel all this. Something tells me Bluelight isn't just trying to build a better solar panel."

"Meanwhile, what will you be doing?"

In the glow of the phone, Nina could see the determined grin on King's face. "I think I'm going to go have a look around."

22.

Pierce gazed down at the still form and marveled at just how human it looked. There were differences of course, most notably, the heavy brow ridge, similar in many respects to depictions of Neanderthal man, to say nothing of the enormous size and the hard looking bumps covering almost every square inch of the creature's body. All but the area between the forehead and the end of the strong aquiline nose, were covered in the bumps.

If not for the bumpy skin, Pierce thought, *you might not give him a second look walking through the mall.*

Oops...make that her.

The archaeologist carefully, almost reverently, extracted the coin from the creature's mouth and held it up for inspection. It was a silver Mexican peso coin, dated 1977. He was almost disappointed that the beasts, intelligent though they were, had chosen such a common and geographically proximal coin to use as an *obol*. He put the peso back, exactly as it had been and moved to the next body in line.

He winced as everything in the objective lens grew painfully bright, and lowered the monocular, blinking away the bright spots. De Bord had entered the chamber, using his flashlight to show the way.

"Damn it," the soldier complained, keeping his voice low in spite of his irritation. "You call this takin' a look? Those things won't take kindly to you violatin' their dead."

"I don't know if they'd care." Pierce slipped the coin from the second corpse's mouth and checked it.

It was most definitely not a peso.

"Well, I'd just as soon focus on gettin' outta here. If they ain't comin' back, then we should keep movin' forward. There's bound to be another opening back to the surface."

Pierce barely heard him. He showed De Bord the coin. Even without being able to translate the strange pictographic writing, the square hole punched in the center of the bronze circle was enough of a clue to identify the coin's country of origin.

"Holy…is that Chinese?"

Pierce nodded. "It's a *banliang* coin, from the Qin Dynasty. This coin is more than two thousand years old."

"How in God's name did it get here?"

Pierce grimaced. "You were right about there being another way out." Pierce said, unable to keep the awe from his voice. "I just hope we don't have to walk that far."

23.

King had done more than his share of covert infiltrations, some more successful than others. Luck played a role, but what really made the difference between an effective sneak-and-peek and a clusterfuck of epic proportions was advanced planning based on reliable intel. With Deep Blue guiding them remotely, updating them with real time satellite imagery or infrared surveillance from an unmanned drone, Chess Team had become masters of stealthy insertion into potentially hostile environments.

King had none of those advantages tonight. No Deep Blue, no eye in the sky, no backup. And perhaps worst of all, no time.

He spent several minutes studying the area surrounding the cinderblock structure that had been the final destination for the driver of the SUV. There didn't appear to be any security cameras or motion sensors, and he saw no evidence of a security patrol. Although he could have been wrong about any one of those observations, there was nothing more to be gained through further surveillance.

"I'd much rather do this alone," he told Nina, then fore-stalled her immediate protest with a raised hand. "I think we both know that it's not a good idea to split up. But you're going to have to follow my lead and do everything I say."

She nodded, but was clearly irked at being relegated to the role of tagalong.

King left the Humvee concealed behind a low hill and they set off on foot across the open ground, a distance of about half a mile. They moved low and slow at first, with King in the lead, constantly scanning for trip wires and other early warning detection systems. As they got closer though, King realized his caution was unnecessary.

The building he now thought of as the Bluelight Facility, might have actually had a working security system at one time, possibly even earlier in the night, but precautions designed to keep out human intruders had been of little use in turning back a wave of Mogollon Monsters.

The eight-foot fence surrounding the building had been ripped apart like the wrapping on an eight-year old's Christmas present. Beyond the fence line, were the shattered remains of two passenger cars, and King saw that the white SUV had also taken a pounding. There were holes in the concrete wall, some decorated with snags of long dark human hair and streaks of blood. The metal door leading inside was still on its hinges, but the exterior doorknob had been ripped off, and it was evident that the panel had been repeatedly hammered with fists and feet.

King led the way through the wreckage and cautiously pulled the door open. The entry foyer beyond was dark, but judging by the lack of damage, it appeared that the creatures had not breached the interior of the building.

A strip of light, barely visible to the naked eye but glowing bright in the night vision display, shone from beneath a door at the end of the corridor. King switched off the monocular, shouldered his carbine, and stealthily approached the door.

There were voices beyond—at least two people—engaged in a conversation. He twisted the doorknob slowly and opened it just a crack.

"—all left when those things attacked. It's just me now." The voice was male—probably Copeland, King thought—and his tone was almost frantic.

"Are you able to verify a direct link between this incursion and activation of the Bluelight generator?" This voice was female and considerably louder, filling the room. King realized right away that it was issuing from a speaker, but there was something odd about the person's speech pattern. There was a barely perceptible lag between each word, and an almost total lack of emotion.

"A link?" Copeland replied incredulously. "Every time we fire the damn thing up, those creatures show up and start killing everyone. What more evidence do you need?"

"There is an eighty-two point one percent probability that these events are correlated. However, until the mechanism explaining the connection is understood, the experiments must continue."

"It sounds like one of those automated phone call systems," Nina whispered in King's ear.

King had already figured that out. Computer voice technology had come a long way from the synthesized speech depicted in movies like the classic *War Games*. Modern software could almost instantly piece together sentences from prerecorded words, assembling them like fragments cut out of a dictionary and pasted onto a sheet of paper, but there were limits to the technology; it was impossible for the software to mimic the natural tone and inflection of a real person. But it was something else the voice had said that caused a huge piece of the puzzle to fall into place.

Oblivious to his revelation, Nina continued. "It sounds like they know that whatever they're doing here is driving the Mogollons crazy."

"Shhh."

"No, no, no! We don't dare turn it on again."

"The objective cannot be achieved until the external threat is mitigated," the female voice replied blandly. "You must accelerate the timetable. Drawing the hostiles into the open will provide military assets with an opportunity to eliminate the threat permanently."

"Those things wiped out your precious military assets. Dozens of soldiers are missing...probably dead. The general blames me for that."

"Blame is irrelevant. Military assets now have a more complete understanding of the threat, and will subsequently escalate their response. There is a seventy-eight point three percent probability that the threat will be completely eliminated within three experimental cycles."

Any lingering doubts King might have had were swept away by the electronically produced voice's second probability assessment. Brainstorm!

Just a few short weeks ago, King had learned of the mysterious entity known as Brainstorm. Hardly anything was known about Brainstorm. Deep Blue had hinted at the possibility that it was in reality an artificial intelligence program that had infiltrated computer networks around the world. It was surreptitiously controlling corporations and governments alike, all to advance an unknown, but almost certainly apocalyptic agenda; King's first encounter with Brainstorm had uncovered a scheme intended to turn literally billions of people into a mindless drone labor force.

During that mission, King had interacted directly with Brainstorm utilizing a similar electronic voice interface that effectively masked the true identity—the true nature—of

Brainstorm, but whatever he, she, it or they was or were, Brainstorm saw the world entirely in terms of probabilities.

Brainstorm didn't think small. Whatever its interest in Bluelight, it almost certainly spelled bad news on a global scale.

"Commence the next activation cycle in forty-seven minutes, and fifteen seconds. Mark."

King immediately pressed a button on his wristwatch, activating the stopwatch function.

"This is insane," Copeland muttered.

"Negative. If your supposition is correct, and the events with hostiles of unknown origin are directly connected to the activation of the Bluelight generator, then repeated aggravation of the hostiles by that method is the only way to ensure their extermination. The Bluelight facility will be adequately protected. Military assets are now aware of the true nature of the threat and will be able to eliminate it more effectively. This is the course of action with the highest probability of success, and will ensure continued operation of the Bluelight generator."

As the electronically produced voice droned on, King began his own probability assessment. He didn't know what Bluelight was, but it was plainly evident that Copeland was critical to its operation.

King eased the door open a little more, and saw the physicist seated at a workstation in a room that looked like a scaled down version of NASA mission control. Copeland was alone.

Take Copeland...or take him out...and Bluelight is dead in the water. Problem solved.

But before he could take that next step, something in his pocket started buzzing like a swarm of angry bees.

Damn it, Aleman. The tech expert should have known better than to call in the middle of an infiltration. King eased the door closed and dug the phone from his pocket.

His heart skipped a beat when he saw the name on the caller ID.

"Who is it?" Nina whispered.

King fought to find his voice as he retreated from the door to the Bluelight control room. "I have to take this."

24.

Pierce and De Bord ran for their lives.

Pierce blamed himself. He had been overconfident in his belief that the creatures would continue to ignore them, and so had ventured further into their subterranean territory than was, he now realized looking back, wise.

It wasn't like they had strolled through the middle of a gathering. In fact, he wasn't sure exactly how they'd gotten by the group of monsters that now stalked them. To the best of his knowledge, they hadn't passed any junctions.

After leaving the burial cave, he and De Bord had continued through the exit passage, in the creatures' wake. Although he secretly hoped to discover more about the strange, almost human beings, Pierce's foremost goal was always to find a way back to the surface. It was plainly evident however that they were descending, deeper and deeper into the Earth's crust. After more than a mile of walking, the cool cave air growing warmer with each vertical foot of drop, Pierce had begun second-guessing the initial decision to move forward.

"This ain't gettin' us anywhere," De Bord had announced, as if tuning into the same psychic channel. "The entry was there. We both went through it. We must've just missed it somehow."

Pierce had been on the verge of agreeing to the request when a glinting reflection caught his eye on the path ahead. "Let me check something out. Five more minutes, then we'll turn back."

De Bord hadn't been happy about it, but he'd nodded, and Pierce had moved ahead into a cavern almost as large as the burial chamber. What he saw there left him speechless. It was, he imagined, the archaeological equivalent of winning the lottery.

It was impossible to say what purpose the room served for the beasts. It might have been the equivalent of a treasure room or perhaps a museum; if they were as intelligent as the totem necklaces seemed to indicate, then it was not beyond the realm of possibility that they might recognize the value in other human artifacts. Or, they might simply have been great big pack rats feathering their nest with anything shiny that caught their eye. Ultimately, the creatures' motivation didn't matter nearly as much as the actual content they had collected.

The room was piled high with artifacts from every part of the globe. Pierce's eye was drawn immediately to something familiar, a pile of bronze armaments—swords, spearheads, helmets—from the early Greek Classical period. But right next to those were gold figurines that looked Meso-American. There was no logic to the arrangement; the only common thread was that all the pieces were metal, specifically metals or alloys that were resistant to corrosion. Reddish and green lumps on the floor marked the resting places of objects of iron and copper that had not survived the passage of centuries…millennia, even.

Yet, it was not the temporal journey of these artifacts that interested Pierce, but rather their physical journey. How had artifacts from civilizations in every corner the globe come to rest here, in this cave in Arizona?

There might have been an explanation for the ancient coins—the *banliang* and the *tetradrachm*—worn by the creatures as amulets. Coins had a way traveling well beyond the borders of their country of origin, and there was plenty of evidence to suggest that ancient mariners had visited the Americas many centuries before Columbus. Coins brought by travelers might have found their way into the underworld. But Pierce had also been entertaining another possibility, and what he saw here seemed to reinforce that theory.

Then De Bord had hastened into the cavern. "They're right behind me," the soldier had shouted, gripping Pierce's shoulder and propelling him forward. "And they're pissed."

And so they had run. Deeper, ever deeper into the Earth.

The creatures, when he happened to glimpse them in the distance, were not driven by the rabid fury that had possessed them during the attack on the camp, but they were nevertheless agitated by the intrusion. Their shrieks multiplied as the sound echoed down the long tunnels, like the cries of the damned rising up from Hell itself. What he could not comprehend, what he dared not even stop to think about, was why they had not already been caught. The creatures were fast, and on their home turf; by all rights, Pierce and De Bord should have been caught a dozen times over.

They're toying with us, Pierce thought. *Some kind of cat-and-mouse game.*

Yet what alternative did they have but to scurry like mice?

"Left or right?" De Bord shouted.

Pierce glanced ahead and saw two diverging tunnels framed in the circle of the soldier's flashlight. It was the first time they'd been confronted with such a choice, and now the enormity of the consequences of making the wrong decision seemed too terrible to contemplate. There were no obvious cues to suggest which path—if either—would lead to safety. Unlike the elaborate ruins he'd had occasion to explore, these passages were the work of nature, carved by flows of water and the vagaries of geology, without any thought for superstitious preferences. It was a coin-flip really.

"Left," he said, barely able to get the words out. "Stay with the main passage."

That it was the wrong choice became evident almost right away. Almost as soon as they passed the opening on the right, the creatures pursuing them let loose with a bone-jarring chorus of shrieks. Then, as if to answer them, a second cacophony erupted from the darkness directly ahead of them. They were caught between two groups of the creatures. De Bord skidded to a halt and raised his carbine, ready to make a desperate last stand.

Pierce glanced back. The monsters chasing them had not closed in, but hung back, cloaked in shadows.

"Back!" Pierce yelled. "We can make it to the other tunnel."

De Bord nodded and with Pierce now leading the way, the two men sprinted back to the diverging tunnel. As soon as they entered it, the creatures lowered their cries, and began advancing again, pushing them forward relentlessly.

The tunnel was cramped, barely large enough for De Bord in his combat gear to make it through, and for a brief instant, Pierce thought maybe the constricting passage would hamper the pursuit. Somehow though, the creatures slipped confidently through the tight confines; both men could hear the scrape of hard knobby skin against stone and the low ululations of the monsters drawing closer all the time.

Then a different noise punctuated their desperate flight, the electronic chirp of Pierce's cell phone.

He dug it out of his pocket automatically, as if he were merely strolling across the campus quad at the university in Athens. The glowing screen displayed the words:

One missed call.

Pierce gasped as the significance of the message hit home. The phone had a signal. That could only mean that they were very close to an opening to the surface. The realization opened a reservoir of strength, and he leaped ahead with renewed urgency, one eye always on the bars indicating the strength of the wireless signal. Fifty steps and a second bar lit up, then a third.

They were close.

With the abruptness of a guillotine slice, the tunnel came to a dead end.

"No!" The denial ripped from Pierce's lips even as he checked the screen again. Three bars still. There had to be an opening here somewhere.

"Climb!" De Bord shouted from behind him. The soldier directed his light to a spot above his head. Instead of bouncing back from the rough basalt, the light revealed an open space.

That was good enough for Pierce. With the agility of a world-class climber, he scrambled up the chimney-like passage, finding handholds and steps in the jagged rock. De Bord was right below him, shining the light straight up now and revealing the narrow slot of an opening just a few more feet above the archaeologist.

Pierce erupted from the hole and onto the desert floor like a dolphin leaping out of the water. He hastily reversed his position and reached down to help De Bord complete his ascent, and a few moments later they were both free of the underground prison.

Pierce scrambled to his feet, ready to start running again, but then he realized that the creatures had left off their wailing. He glanced at De Bord. "I think we're okay," he said, uncertainly. "I think they were just trying to run us off."

The soldier blinked at him, then cautiously played his light over the hole from which they had emerged. There was no sign of the creatures.

Pierce sat down wearily, resting his head against his knees.

De Bord sat next to him, shaking his head. "I sure as hell didn't sign up for that," he said with a forced chuckle. "Any idea where we are?"

Pierce checked his phone again. There was a GPS application that would pinpoint their exact location, but that was the last thing on his mind. King had tried to call, and that meant his friend was still alive. The implications of the discoveries he had made in the underworld lair of the creatures seemed insignificant compared to that.

He touched his finger to the screen, bringing up King's number, and then tapped it again to send the call.

There was an interminably long delay before a familiar voice said: "George?"

The sound of King's voice triggered a wave of relief. "Jack! Thank God."

"What the hell happened to you? Are you all right?"

"Yeah. There was a minute or two where I wasn't so sure, but…Jack, you're not going to believe what I've found."

"You can tell me all about it when I get there. Where are you?"

25.

Ivan Sokoloff scanned the hills with his night vision device, watching for his target's approach.

Always a consummate professional, he had never once treated any hit as easy money, and despite his failure in New York, he had not made that mistake with this one last job. But never in his wildest dreams could he have imagined a hunt like this. He almost considered demanding more money for the job, but would his mysterious employer really believe his tale of inhuman monsters?

Probably not.

Sokoloff sighed wearily. At least it was almost over now. He'd picked up the trail of King's friend, George Pierce, confident that the archaeologist would lead him to his quarry, and his patience was about to be rewarded. Although barely visible against the night sky, he caught a glimpse of a dust cloud rising over the crest of a hill less than half a mile away. A moment later, the silhouette of a military truck rolled into view and then proceeded down the exposed flank.

It seemed to take Pierce a little while longer to make out the approaching Humvee, but as the vehicle drew closer, the man got to his feet, presumably in anticipation of the impending reunion.

Sokoloff smiled, thinking about the ten million dollars he was about to earn. He lowered the night vision device, hefted the weapon he had earlier appropriated, and then, in his best approximation of a Texas accent, said: "Well, I reckon it's time you introduce me to this buddy of yours."

26.

King glanced at the glowing numbers on his watch and then at the display on his phone, which showed Pierce's location as a dot almost right on top of the dot that showed his own. Almost twenty minutes had passed since he'd gotten Pierce's call; in less than half an hour, Copeland would activate the Bluelight generator—whatever that was—and in all likelihood trigger another attack from the Mogollon Monsters.

The decision to leave Bluelight and retrieve his friend had been one of the hardest King had ever made. He'd thought about it for almost a full minute, which was an eternity for the decisive, highly analytical Chess Team field leader.

Shutting down Bluelight might have been as easy as stepping through the door to the control room and telling Copeland to stand down. Given the physicist's reluctance to continue the experiment, he probably would have complied eagerly. But then again, there was every possibility that he would have been unable to stop the generator from being activated. Brainstorm probably had contingency plans in place against just such a breakdown of his control, and without understanding more about Bluelight and how it worked, there was no guarantee that King could actually prevent the next activation cycle. And if he had tried and failed, there was no guarantee that Pierce would survive another rampage. On the other hand, there was just enough time for him to exit the Bluelight compound, rendezvous with Pierce, and make it back before Copeland threw the switch. If he could pull that off, it would be win-win, so while there was a degree of risk involved, it was clearly the preferable course of action.

But what if I'm wrong? What if more people die because I put my personal feelings ahead of the mission?

He knew better than to ask "what-if" questions.

Pierce had reappeared on the eastern flank of the Superstitions, almost two miles to the north of the FOB where they had briefly been held, and only about five miles from the Bluelight facility. Ideally, even at off-road speeds, the round trip should have taken no more than about twenty minutes, and that had probably influenced his decision as well. Unfortunately, the landscape had decided not to be cooperative. He had anticipated that the rough terrain would slow him down and restrict his ability to drive in a straight line. Some of the undulating hills were low enough that he could simply drive up and over, while the steeper ones, those that couldn't be surmounted, were circumvented. What he had failed to take into account was that Mother Nature was not the only force shaping the topography. About a mile from the Bluelight facility, he spotted a smooth, dark area directly in his path. At a distance, it looked like a lake, but as they drew closer the air filled with the pungent rotten-egg smell of sulfur dioxide, and he recognized it for what it was: the sludge pond for the copper processing plant.

Finding a way to detour around the toxic pool added another seven minutes to the journey, and to get around it, he had to drive across the sloping flanks of the hills that formed a natural bowl in which the mine operators had chosen to dump the byproducts of the ore separation process. There were more than a few hairy moments where the Humvee started sliding, forcing him to steer up the hill until the wheels found purchase. And all the while, the clock kept ticking.

On the far side of the bowl, he pointed the front end of the Humvee up the hill and pressed down on the accelerator. The tires slipped a little, throwing out an unseen cloud of dust, and then the truck grudgingly started climbing up and over the crest. As they rolled over the top, King spotted a bright glow directly ahead; a small light, amplified to blazing intensity by his night vision.

"There's George," he said.

Nina didn't respond, and he wasn't sure if she had heard him over the engine noise, but a moment later she shifted forward in her seat and peered out into the darkness. With the unaided eye, the light probably wasn't visible, and by King's best guess, they were still a good quarter-mile away, with a long, winding valley between them and Pierce.

Despite being built for such conditions, the Humvee bounced and slipped precariously as they raced along the sloping hillside, bumping over large rocks, dodging enormous saguaro cacti and crushing smaller desert flora. As the driver, he was only slightly better able to anticipate the violent jolts; Nina was being mercilessly tossed around in her seat. Nevertheless, King maintained steady pressure on the accelerator pedal, eager to reunite with his friend, and all too painfully aware of the fact that the impending activation of the Bluelight device was about to unleash another wave of hell on earth.

But then, with only about a hundred yards separating them from the glowing orb of light that marked what he presumed to be Pierce's location, King slammed on the brakes. The Humvee skidded sideways as the natural decline of the hill redirected some of its momentum.

"What's wrong?" Nina shouted.

King's eyes never wavered from his goal. "George has company."

27.

Pierce felt a moment of apprehension when he spied the approaching Humvee, but quickly reasoned that King had somehow utilized his military connections to get some assistance from the troops in the area.

When the truck finally stopped in front of him and two soldiers climbed out, their rifles at the ready, he realized his mistake. One of the men stalked over to where he and De Bord were waiting and addressed the sergeant.

"What's the story here?"

De Bord seemed a little confused by the turn of events. "Ah, this is one of the hikers we picked up. We got separated from the rest during the attack."

"You were at FOB Apache?" There was a hint of awe in the soldier's voice. "We didn't think anyone survived."

"Yeah, it was pretty bad," De Bord remarked.

Pierce sagged in disappointment as he realized that King was not accompanying the soldiers, and worse, that he was now evidently a prisoner again.

"I better call this in," the soldier said. He turned to his companion. "Take the civilian into custody. We need to get back ASAP."

A third soldier, occupying the roof turret of the parked Humvee suddenly shouted: "Sergeant! We've got another truck rolling up."

Pierce reflexively followed the gunner's line of sight, but could only make out a dust cloud and a dark speck moving against the terrain.

"What the hell? There's not supposed to be anyone else out here." The sergeant in charge climbed into the truck and started talking into the radio, but the remaining soldier advanced on Pierce.

"He's really moving!"

The gunner's shout seemed only to add to the confusion, and for a few more seconds, all the soldiers, including De Bord, seemed paralyzed by indecision. That was all the time the driver of the approaching Humvee needed to close the gap.

The vehicle, outfitted with a canvas-covered cargo area, drove right up alongside the others steering straight toward Pierce and the others, as if it meant to run them down. At the last instant, Pierce was yanked away, in front of the parked Humvee, while De Bord scrambled in the other direction.

Amidst the confusion, the passenger door of the still rolling vehicle flew open, and Pierce found himself staring at the familiar face of Nina Raglan.

"Get in!"

28.

Sokoloff spat out a curse in Russian, along with a mouthful of dirt, as he watched the Humvee pull away. This job just kept getting worse.

The roar of a machine gun punctuated the sentiment. The turret gunner had opened up with his M240B and Sokoloff saw white tracers arc across the desert in pursuit of the retreating vehicle. It looked like a few of the rounds found their mark, but the Humvee continued picking up speed, and a few moments later, vanished around the edge of a hillside.

As the gun fell silent, Sokoloff heard some shouting and realized the words were directed at him. He looked up and found the sergeant in charge of the group standing over him. "Come on! In the truck! Let's…"

Sokoloff saw the change in the man's eyes, saw his lips continue moving to form a word even after his voice had trailed off.

"You aren't De—"

Sokoloff jammed the muzzle of his carbine under the soldier's chin and squeezed the trigger.

He was up and moving before the man's body hit the dirt, dashing to the idle Humvee. The violence of his actions took the remaining soldiers completely off guard. The sergeant died from a contact shot to the forehead, the radio handset still pressed to one ear and a confused look on his face. The gunner, possibly unaware of anything that had transpired since the other Humvee's escape, flinched a little when he heard the shot, but the tight confines of the circular turret opening made it impossible for him to see what was going on inside his own vehicle, much less respond when Sokoloff shoved his carbine up under the soldier's body armor and fired off several more rounds.

With brutal efficiency and indifference, Sokoloff hauled the bodies of his latest victims out of the truck and left them on the desert floor, just as he had done earlier with the two-man patrol back on the hiking trail—the real Sergeant De Bord and another young man whose name he hadn't bothered to learn.

He then climbed back into the Humvee and started the engine. There was yet more killing to be done before the night was through.

29.

As they rounded a turn in the ravine, the incessant crack of 7.62 mm rounds on the truck's frame ceased immediately, but King still had to shout to be heard over the roaring engine.

"Anyone hit?"

Pierce and Nina, crowded together in the footwell on the passenger side, both signaled that they were all right.

"Hang on!"

King drove like a man possessed. Another encounter with the Army was the last thing he had expected, and it added one more variable to an already complicated equation. He checked the side mirror, but with the hillside in the way, it was impossible to know if the soldiers were giving chase. He assumed they were.

Pierce, still panting from the burst of excitement, disentangled from Nina. "You guys aren't going to believe the night I've had."

"Try me," Nina replied with a laugh.

King glanced over. As urgent as their present situation was, he couldn't discount the possibility that Pierce might have gleaned some important bit of information. "Let's hear it, George."

In a rush, Pierce told of his escape from the camp and subsequent fall into the underground labyrinth. Nina questioned him about the behavior of the Mogollon Monsters—how they had initially ignored Pierce and De Bord, and then chased them out of the cave.

"It was like they were herding us," Pierce confessed. "They could have caught us at any time, but they didn't. It was like they were just trying to show us the door."

"It makes sense," Nina said. "They're normally very shy. They don't like getting close too people. The only reason they've been attacking is because of that Bluelight thing."

"Bluelight?"

"I'll tell you about that in a minute," King said. "Finish your story."

"Right. You aren't going to believe this, but I think the caves we were in are connected to a much, much bigger network."

Nina nodded. "There are a lot of people who think that's the case. There have always been stories about a cave system under the Superstitions and stretching at least as far as the Grand Canyon, with entrances that periodically appear and then vanish. According to one legend, Geronimo escaped from a troop of cavalry scouts by seemingly stepping into the rocks—a cave entrance—but the soldiers couldn't find it afterward."

"I think these caves might connect a lot further than that. I found artifacts from civilizations all over the world. There might be an entire undiscovered world down there, a fully functioning ecosystem with its own evolutionary pathway. Maybe even civilizations. Those creatures are intelligent; they have a complex set of behaviors that are far more advanced than any animal species, except of course, humans. Particularly death rituals.

"There's a researcher in Colorado, Jeff Long, who has proposed the theory that a global cave network might be the explanation for all our myths relating to the existence of an afterlife under the ground. Hell, Hades, Sheol, Xibalba…call it what you will, every civilization has a belief in an underworld."

"That would also explain why reports of similar creatures show up in different parts of the world," Nina said. "And why it's been so hard to verify their existence. They come up for air once in a while, and then duck back down into their own world."

"There could be thousands of them," Pierce agreed. "Millions perhaps. And now for some reason, they've declared war on us." He paused a beat. "So, what's Bluelight?"

King was about to answer when he spied a pair of lights in the distance directly ahead. The beams were diffuse, and despite of the amplification from his PVS-7 they weren't blindingly bright.

Blackout drive lights.

Because so many military operations were conducted under cover of darkness, all Humvees were equipped with a second set of lights, designed specifically to work with night vision, bright enough to illuminate the surroundings without rendering night vision devices useless, but practically invisible to the unaided eye, even at a distance of only a few feet. King hadn't used the blackout lights in their vehicle because doing so would have betrayed their presence to the roving patrols.

He didn't think it was the same group of soldiers that had caught Pierce. This vehicle—also a hard-shelled M1026 HMMWV configured as a gunship, with a crew-served machine gun—was directly ahead and moving toward them from a different position. He surmised that a call had gone out, warning of a renegade Humvee roaming the hills. That meant there was one still behind them.

"More company," he warned. Pierce and Nina both ducked, as if his observation had been accompanied by another volley of machine gun fire.

King sorted through his mental map of the terrain. He had a pretty good idea where he was in relation to the Bluelight facility, and that remained his primary objective. Evading the troops now searching for him wouldn't count for much if the facility went active again. The problem was, the Humvee now approaching was directly between him and where he wanted to be.

Maybe not a problem after all, he thought, punching the accelerator. The Humvee quickly picked up speed and began bouncing violently across the landscape, He knew it would take the soldiers in the other truck a few seconds to realize what he was doing, and hopefully a few seconds more to decide how best to respond.

He decided to give them exactly six seconds, and started counting "Mississippis" under his breath. When he got to six, with probably no more than seventy-five yards separating the two vehicles, he flipped his PVS-7 up, away from his eye, and switched on the headlights.

Twin halogen beams speared out across the dusty darkness and transfixed the second Humvee. He knew from experience what a bright light could do to a night vision device and to the person wearing it; the flash would have overloaded the electronics of a PVS-7 type device, rendering it useless for several hours thereafter, but in the instant before that happened, the wearer would feel like he'd stared directly at the sun. The wearer's other, unaided eye wouldn't fare much better; with pupils dilated for maximum natural night vision, any flash of light would be painful and would leave an imprint like fireworks on the retinas for at least several minutes thereafter.

The trick with the lights hadn't done his own night vision any favors. King switched the headlights off right away, and lowered his PVS-7 into place.

The two Humvees were still on a collision course, separated by only a few yards. The only reason that they hadn't already crashed was that the other driver, possibly blinded, had let his foot off the accelerator and tapped the brakes.

King swerved hard right. The Humvee skidded into the turn and the back driver's side wheel banged off the front bumper of the other truck. There was a crunch as the fiberglass hood cover splintered but the damage was purely cosmetic. The impact knocked King's Humvee back around and it scraped along the side of the gunship, but then they were past, and back on course.

There was a staccato eruption behind them, a sound like a car backfiring repeatedly, and King ducked. "Stay down."

It didn't sound like any of the rounds had hit. King hoped the gunner was literally firing blind, strafing the general area where he thought they were, using the "spray and pray" method. The problem was, sometimes that method worked.

He kept going, taking as much speed as the vehicle and terrain would let him have, following the descending flank of a hillside in hopes that it would take them out of the line of fire.

A glance at the side mirror revealed nothing—not the absence of pursuit, but rather the absence of the mirror itself. Evidently, it had been a casualty of the sideswipe. King risked poking his head out the window, and saw lights moving behind them. The crew of the M1026 had eschewed blackout mode and were now running with full lights. They were also turning around.

King glanced at his watch. Thirty-six minutes had elapsed since he and Nina had left the Bluelight facility. In about ten more, it would activate again, summoning a fresh horde of Mogollon Monsters to assault anything that moved. He dug out his phone and brought up the GPS app. He'd marked the Bluelight facility as a waypoint earlier. According to the app, it was now about three miles dead ahead.

The Humvee bounced and slid, and King had to wrestle with the steering wheel to maintain a semblance of control as he climbed hills and shot straight down the slopes. Behind him, the lights of the pursuing vehicle blazed like tiny suns. The driver of the M1026 couldn't close the gap; both Humvees were traveling well beyond the recommended off-road speed, and nearly at the limit of what was possible, but the pursuing truck had one significant advantage. They could reach out across the distance and ruin King's day. The arc of tracer fire, sporadically ricocheting off the desert floor, sometimes too close for comfort, indicated that they were trying to do exactly that.

As King climbed a steep slope, he heard more bullets hammer against the metal deck of the rear cargo area. The gunner was dialing in on them and it was only a matter of time before rounds starting tearing through the fabric covering the cab.

"Enough of this shit," King rasped. He tore off his borrowed helmet and the PVS-7 with it, and turned the headlights on again. There was no sense in trying to do what he had to do next in near total darkness.

He kept the accelerator to the floor, ignoring the deafening roar of the overburdened diesel engine, until the truck crested the hill. For an instant, the Humvee's tires lost contact and it sailed through air, traveling almost thirty feet before finally crunching onto the downslope. Pierce and Nina were pitched about the interior like bits of popcorn, but King ignored their curses. His attention was focused on the glistening mirror-like surface that stretched out directly in front of him.

King hadn't forgotten about the sludge pond, but as the Humvee bounced twice more, traveling another fifty feet down the hill even though he now had the brake pedal pressed to the floor, he realized that he might have been a little too eager to reach it. After the third bounce, the wheels remained in contact with the ground and the truck slid forward several more yards before finally coming to rest with its front end jutting out over the toxic pool.

There wasn't even a second to waste on a sigh of relief. King threw the gear selector into 'reverse,' cranked the wheel forty-five degrees, and brought the truck around so that it was facing up hill at an angle. He had just shifted back into 'drive' when the chasing Humvee erupted off the crest of the hill.

He caught a glimpse of the other vehicle's headlights, shining out through the dust cloud like spotlights searching the sky, but then the beams dipped down to illuminate the sludge pond. King's Humvee rolled forward, traversing the slope diagonally, as the pursuing vehicle bounced and skidded straight into the sulfur dioxide tainted pool. King didn't hear the splash, but knew that the truck had failed to stop in time when the headlights vanished.

As he sped along the edge of the bowl, King half expected to see more Humvees taking up the chase, but that was the least of his worries. He kept one eye on the GPS display, watching as the dots moved closer to each other, but he stopped checking his watch. He didn't need it to tell him that he had probably made the wrong decision by going to retrieve Pierce. He wasn't going to make it back to Bluelight in time.

Then, as if in answer to his prayers, the cinder block building appeared in the distance as he crested a hill. The beam of his headlights revealed a lot more than he had glimpsed earlier. Just beyond the structure, a ragged edge cut across the landscape in either direction, further than the eye could see. The Bluelight facility was perched on the edge of the abandoned open-pit mine.

Beyond that hill, the remaining distance was relatively flat, and after about two hundred yards, the Humvee crossed the rutted dirt that led directly to the fenced compound. The moment the tires transitioned onto the road, the ride instantly smoothed out, allowing Nina and Pierce to emerge from their huddle.

King looked over at them. They both looked like they had been trapped in a tumble dryer. "Still with me?"

Pierce gave a half-hearted laugh. "Let's not do that again."

"No more off-road," King promised. "You have my word on that. We're almost there."

"How much time do we have?" Nina asked.

King glanced at his watch, knowing that he wouldn't like what he saw there. The chronometer had just ticked past 46:15. "Not enough."

Maybe not enough to stop Bluelight from activating, but if he could get to Copeland and convince the physicist to shut it down…

The thought slipped away as the headlights lit up the building, and he saw that they had another problem. Arrayed in a semi-circle, just beyond the fenced area, were half a dozen M1026s, bristling with M240B and Browning M2 .50-caliber machine guns.

The Army had come to protect Bluelight.

King kept driving forward, but his foot eased off the accelerator. Fancy driving wasn't going to get him past this obstacle. At about a hundred yards, he braked to a stop and shut down the vehicle. As if waiting for that cue, a team of soldiers, advanced on foot, keeping their carbines trained on the new arrivals.

"Shit," Nina whispered. "What do we do now?"

King didn't have an answer. After all they had gone through to get back, he wasn't about to be stopped at the finish line, but he had no idea how they were going to overcome this last hurdle. He was still trying to think of something inspiring to say when the area just behind the cinder block structure lit up with a blue glow.

FUSION

30.

East of Phoenix, Arizona — 1026 UTC (3:25 am Local)

After five minutes of fruitless searching, Sokoloff knew that he had lost his prey. In the maze of hills and valleys, there were any number of possible paths, and it was evident that King had taken one and he had somehow wandered down another. Only pride had prevented him from contacting his employer to ask for assistance—specifically, the GPS location of George Pierce's cell phone—but he wasn't foolish enough to let pride stand in the way of finishing the job and earning his ten million dollars.

He was a little dismayed to discover that he'd received three text messages, presumably sent during the time he'd been underground with Pierce. The first was an almost polite request for an update. The second was more direct, almost demanding in tone, but essentially a repeat of the first, with an urgent appeal to execute the contract as soon as possible. The third, now almost ten minutes old, was a variation on the blackmail threat that had been used to draw him out of retirement. If the message was to be believed, Interpol was already hot on his trail.

Sokoloff sighed. He didn't think his employer was that rash, and he couldn't imagine why, all of a sudden, it had become critical to rush the job to completion, but if that was really how it was going to play out, then so be it. He had eluded the authorities before, and he could do it again if necessary.

But maybe it wouldn't be necessary.

Skipping the tedious step of sending a reply, Sokoloff dialed the number from which the messages had been sent. The call connected immediately.

"You have broken protocol." The voice was female, but sounded artificial like an automated answering service. He half expected to be instructed to press "1" to continue in English. Instead, the voice went on. "Please provide an explanation for the lapse in communication, and your subsequent decision to initiate direct voice contact."

"I am sick of trying to type on this thing," Sokoloff snarled. "If you're so worried about getting this job done right away, stop jerking me around with text messages."

"Your objection to established methods of communication has been noted. Please provide an explanation for the lapse in communication."

"I went through a tunnel and lost the signal. It doesn't matter. What matters is that I need you to track Pierce again. The target is close by, but I can't find him. Tell me where Pierce is, and I'll end this."

"George Pierce is currently one point six miles east of your location, traveling at an average speed of forty-two miles per hour."

Sokoloff sighed again. "Just send his coordinates to my phone in real-time."

"Negative. There is an eighty-nine point seven percent probability that the target is en route to a known location. The coordinates for that location have been sent. Proceed there immediately and execute the contract without further delay."

"How do you know where he's going?"

There was no answer. The call had been terminated at the other end. Sokoloff glanced at the screen and saw that his GPS app had been activated to show his new destination.

31.

King got out with his hands raised in a gesture of surrender, but as the soldiers swarmed around him, he said: "You need to let me speak to whoever is in command. It's urgent."

He knew they would eventually accede to his request; it was just a question of how long it would take and how uncomfortable they would choose to make him in the interval.

The soldiers already seemed to grasp the need for urgency. King and the others were manhandled away from the Humvee and rushed back to the fenced area near the entrance to the facility. As they got close, King could feel cobwebs of static electricity brushing his skin and he smelled a whiff of ozone in the air, but the concrete building eclipsed his view of the strange light show that seemed to be issuing from the mine beyond.

"Sigler? I'll be damned, is that you?"

King swung around to meet the source of the familiar voice. "Colonel Mayfield?" He did a double-take when he noticed the star on the man's body armor vest. "Sorry, General Mayfield."

When King had been a platoon leader in the Army Rangers, Colonel Scott Mayfield had been his battalion commander. Mayfield had approved his transfer to Special Forces Operational Detachment Delta, which had been a stepping stone to Chess Team. He remembered Mayfield as an even-tempered and fair commanding officer, but he had no idea what to expect here and now.

The general stalked forward, a hint of frustration in his eyes. "I take it you're the one who's been dogging my men all night. I should have been kept in the loop on Delta activities in my AO."

"I guess you didn't get the memo," King replied. He nearly told the man he wasn't with Delta anymore, but didn't see how that revelation would help the current situation. Better to let him think he was on duty. "And we really don't have time to play catch-up." He took a breath, and then with as much respect as he could muster, said: "Sir, you've got to shut Bluelight down, immediately."

Mayfield shook his head. "Those aren't my orders."

"Then let me talk to Copeland."

The general frowned. "Son, I don't think you grasp the big picture here."

"King!" Nina shouted. "It's starting."

King glanced back at her and saw what looked like a glistening fuzz seeping out the ground around her feet. He turned back to Mayfield. "With all due respect, sir, believe me when I say that I see a lot more of the picture than you. If you don't shut Bluelight down immediately, more of your men are going to die. Let me talk to Copeland. He'll understand."

Mayfield pursed his lips. "I'll let you say your piece, but my orders stand. The Bluelight experiment needs to be completed, and any resulting hostile incursion dealt with and eliminated."

"Then you already know." Nina took a step closer. "You know that it's driving the creatures to the surface, turning them into killers."

Mayfield ignored her and gestured to the door. "This way."

The mist continued to swell out of the ground, sparkling like reflected moonlight, as they stepped into the still darkened foyer. Mayfield barked an order to a subordinate then stepped past King and the others to lead the way to the mission control room.

Not much had changed in the forty-eight minutes since King and Nina had last seen the facility. The only difference was that this time, they didn't linger at the door.

"Dr. Copeland," Mayfield called. "These people would like to speak with you."

The physicist glanced up from his workstation. He looked like a man on the verge of psychotic break. Sweat beaded on his balding pate, and his shirt was rumpled and soiled, as if he hadn't changed it in days. "You're kidding right? Now, of all times?"

King pushed forward. "Dr. Copeland, you have to shut Bluelight down immediately."

"Believe me, I'd love to." Copeland turned back to his computer screen as if there was nothing more to say on the matter.

King wanted to grab the man by the shoulders and shake him, but he kept his anger in check. "I don't think you understand what your device is doing."

Copeland looked up again. "Who are you again? And how do you know anything about Bluelight?"

"I know that it's driving those creatures insane, and I know that as long as you run that machine, they're going to keep coming and they're going to keep killing."

Copeland shook his head. "There have been some unexpected side-effects, but General Mayfield assures me he can deal with that."

"General Mayfield has no idea what Bluelight is doing."

Mayfield didn't hold back. "Sigler, I think you're the one who's clueless here. Do you even realize what Bluelight means for us?"

King didn't have an answer.

"The President has ordered the Defense Department to phase out petroleum usage, and shift to alternate energy productions. Just imagine that. Imagine trying to fight a war from a forward operating base surrounded by fields of windmills and solar panels. It's a strategic nightmare. But Bluelight can change all that."

"Just what in the hell is Bluelight, anyway?" Pierce intoned.

Copeland checked his screen again then stood up. "So you don't know. What a surprise. In a nutshell, it's free energy.

"The Earth is surrounded by a shell of antimatter particles. They're created by the sun and radiate outward in the solar wind. The Earth's magnetic field scoops them up, one antiproton at a time, and there they stay until they eventually decay. In some areas, where the magnetic field is especially strong, there are large anomalies, but you can find them almost everywhere if you know where to look."

"You're harvesting antimatter?" Nina said. "Sounds like something from Star Trek."

Copeland seemed to take that as a compliment. "We don't harvest it. The Bluelight system fires a proton beam into the magnetic field. The protons and antiprotons annihilate each other, just like in the warp core reactor, and produce charged plasma high above the atmosphere. The plasma throws off a lot of loose electrons, which conduct back to the source. We use the lightning to charge an array of batteries. In just eight minutes, the prototype Bluelight device can produce enough electricity to run a small city for an entire day."

Mayfield nodded. "A portable version, small enough to fit in the back of a truck, could power an entire army base. So you see, shutting it down is not an option."

"Don't you realize what's at stake here?" King persisted. "Those creatures are going to keep coming."

"We're ready for them this time. There can't be that many of them left." Mayfield cocked his head sideways. "Wait, is that why you're here? Trying to protect endangered species, or some crap like that?"

As if to underscore his statement, a soldier stepped into the room from the foyer. "Sir, we've engaged the hostiles. And there's something else."

The building must have been heavily insulated, because until the door opened, King hadn't heard any noise from outside. Now, the room was filled with the percussions of thunder and gunfire.

"On my way," Mayfield said. As he reached the door, he turned to King again. "I've got soldier work to do. You three stay here and keep out of Dr. Copeland's way. Bluelight stays on. End of story."

32.

Sokoloff was only half a mile from his goal, when the GPS display blinked off and was replaced by the message:

Signal Lost.

An instant later, the mist started to rise from the ground. The urgency in his employer's demand made a lot more sense. Earlier, the mist had preceded the appearance of the creatures by only a few seconds. The hitman stomped the accelerator to the floor and focused his attention on the building directly ahead.

A bolt of lightning bisected the horizon right in front of him. He winced, blinded momentarily, but kept going. Another flash followed, simultaneous with the boom of thunder from the first, and in the instant where the sky lit up like daylight, he saw shapes emerging from the mist.

An unfamiliar tingle of panic rippled through Sokoloff's body. He had squared off against some of the deadliest men on the planet, and always emerged victorious, but these animals were nothing like his human prey. Executing the contract—killing King and earning ten million dollars—suddenly didn't seem nearly as important as just reaching the safety of the building. Of course, there was no guarantee of safety there…or anywhere.

A dark shape rose up in front of him. He ducked instinctively as the Humvee thudded into the creature, knocking it up onto the hood and against the windshield. Dazed, but probably not dead, the creature blocked his view of the road ahead. There was another thump and the right side of the truck bounced into the air as the wheels rolled over an obstacle that hadn't been there a moment before. The jolt was enough to dislodge the creature on the hood and it rolled to the side, just as another lightning bolt stabbed out the sky.

The creatures were all around him now. Dozens ran ahead of him, seemingly oblivious to his approach. Others came up alongside and slapped at the aluminum exterior of the Humvee, as if trying to grab onto it and hold it in place. Sokoloff wiggled the steering wheel back and forth, knocking the creatures back, as he raced headlong into a hellstorm.

The muzzle flash of machine gun alerted him to the presence of soldiers guarding the facility. He hoped that they would believe him to be one of their own and use their firepower to give him cover for his mad dash; the alternative was too terrible to contemplate.

As he closed the gap, he left the trailing creatures behind and came up on the vanguard. Lost in their primal rage, three of the beasts went under his tires, and then he was in the clear. A few of the soldiers waved him on frantically, little suspecting that he had already killed five of their comrades, and would kill as many more as it took to accomplish the contract. He aimed the truck for a gap between two of the parked Humvees and skidded to a halt, surrounded by a score of stridently cracking carbines and light machine guns.

As he got out, one of the riflemen scrambled up into the turret of his vehicle and got behind the machine gun mounted there. Sokoloff ignored him, and was himself ignored as the soldiers gave their full attention to the advancing threat. Sokoloff made a show of looking for a target, even as he melted back from the skirmish line. King and the others were nowhere to be seen, but the abandoned Humvee he had passed on the way in was evidence enough that his target was nearby. If King wasn't out here, then there was only one place he could be.

The hitman took one last look around to ensure that he wasn't being observed, and then ducked through the doorway.

33.

As the door closed, plunging them back into silence, King tried again. "Dr. Copeland, I overheard your conversation with Brainstorm. We both know that you need to shut it down, at least until you can understand these other effects. That's all I'm asking."

Copeland started at the mention of Brainstorm, but then sagged back into his chair. "What difference would it make now? The general is right; the soldiers will mop up those creatures and that will be the end of it."

"And if he's wrong?" Pierce said. "I've been down there, in the caves where they live. There aren't just a few, or even a few dozen. There might be thousands of them, and your machine is calling them like a dog whistle. How long do you think those soldiers can last against an onslaught like that?"

"They only have to last eight and a half minutes," Copeland sighed.

King leaned down to look the physicist in the eye. "That's twice now you've mentioned eight minutes."

"We don't want to run Bluelight longer than that. With each proton annihilation, the local atmosphere heats up. If it gets hot enough, the gases in the atmosphere will spontaneously enter a state of runaway fusion. If that started, the Earth's atmosphere would catch on fire."

Nina was incredulous. "Oh, you have got to be kidding. It never occurred to you that this might be a bad idea?"

"The thermal effects are completely manageable. I monitor the temperature constantly throughout the process to ensure that it never goes anywhere near critical. Eight and a half minutes is the upper limit of the green zone. It's this other thing that—"

The sudden cacophony of battle indicated to them all that someone had just entered the control room. King glanced over at the approaching soldier and wondered how the battle was going. "That other thing has taken dozens of lives. You've got to stop it, right now. You've surely got enough data to figure what it is about the process that drives these creatures nuts. Shut it down until you can come up with a fix."

Copeland nodded slowly, and King knew he'd finally gotten through to the man. He placed a reassuring hand on the physicist's shoulder and turned his chair around to face the computer terminal.

He heard Pierce speak to the soldier who had just entered. "Sergeant De Bord?"

Two voices spoke, almost at exactly the same moment. The first was the electronically produced and amplified female voice of Brainstorm. "Dr. Copeland, you must disregard Mr. Sigler's request. A complete activation cycle is the only way to ensure that the threat is neutralized."

The second voice was completely unfamiliar. "My apologies, Dr. Pierce, but I fear I have misled you. I am not De Bord."

Something about the Russian accent sent a chill down King's spine.

34.

King knew without looking that the newcomer was pointing a weapon at him. "Just tell me one thing," he said. "Is this guy working for you?"

There was a pause, and for a fleeting second, King feared he'd read the scene wrong. Then Brainstorm responded. "Whom are you addressing, Mr. Sigler?"

"Who do you think? This is all your show, right? The remote-control puppet master? I know that you're the money behind Bluelight. I just want to know if you're also the reason I've got a gang of Russian hitmen chasing me all over the country." King turned slowly toward the ersatz soldier. "I only ask because if he pulls the trigger like I think he's about to, he's just as likely to kill Copeland. Now, if he's not working for you..."

"You have made a valid point, Mr. Sigler. Mr. Sokoloff, please avoid doing anything that might harm Dr. Copeland."

King breathed a silent sigh of relief that his hunch had been right. Brainstorm had been behind the attempted killing in New York, and now it seemed his hired assassin was here to finish the job. He recognized the man's name. Ivan Sokoloff was probably the most notorious hitman ever to have lived, with an alleged body count of nearly five hundred victims. Officially, he'd been found murdered, but many had suspected what King now knew to be the truth: he had faked his death and gone underground.

He seized on this slim advantage, turning to Copeland. "I bet you didn't realize the kind of people you're dealing with. Your research is safe, DARPA will fund you, but you can't take your orders from Brainstorm anymore. Shut it down."

"Dr. Copeland, you have your instructions," Brainstorm said quickly. "Allow the test to continue."

"No," Copeland seemed to sit up a little straighter. "He's right. This is insane. We should have suspended operations after the first incident. I'm turning Bluelight off."

"Dr. Copeland, if you continue with this course of action, it will be necessary to compel you with the threat of lethal force."

"Lethal…?"

"Mr. Sokoloff, if he does not move away from the workstation immediately, you are authorized—"

The end of the threat was lost as the report of Sokoloff's M4 filled the room. Blood sprayed across the computer screen and Copeland slumped forward, his head smashing into the keyboard.

King reacted instantly, diving over the desk as Sokoloff triggered another burst. The 5.56 millimeter rounds scorched the air where he'd been standing. He shouted, "Run!" and then kept moving, scrambling for cover, but there weren't many places to hide and the exits were all completely exposed.

King's mind clicked into combat mode; everything he saw was evaluated on its potential for use as a defensive weapon or to provide cover against incoming fire. Unfortunately, the cheap pressboard desks and tables didn't offer much of either, and he realized he was going to need some kind of miracle to stay alive.

What he got was no miracle.

35.

Pierce kicked himself for not having seen through the phony soldier's fake accent. But never in his wildest dreams would he have imagined that one of the Russians who had attacked them in New York, would follow them here, masquerade as a soldier and then actually help him survive a foray into the underworld, all in an effort to get closer to King.

When the first shot was fired, he grabbed Nina's hand and pulled her down behind a table. He heard King's admonition to run, but there didn't seem to be anywhere to go. Still, putting a little distance between them and the gunman seemed like a good idea.

The door burst open and over the incessant crack of thunder, a bone-chilling wail filled the room. Pierce suddenly realized that taking a bullet had just become a secondary concern. Out of the corner of his eye, he saw three of the towering hairy creatures rush into the room, eyes red with rabid fury. With Nina's hand still locked in his, Pierce zigzagged through the maze of workstations, racing for the door at the far end of the room. Behind him, the crunch of wood and plastic being demolished indicated that the invading creatures were taking a more direct route.

Pierce flung open the door and rushed through into the middle of a dimly lit hallway. There was an exit sign to the right, but going back outside was a frying pan to fire proposition, so he veered left. There were several closed doors lining the hall, and Pierce tried the knob of the first one he came to. Locked.

"Find one that's open," he shouted. "I'll take the left side."

Nina dashed past him to test the doors on the right side of the hall, while he moved down to the next. Locked again.

"Got one!"

At almost the same instant that Nina shouted, the door back to the control room exploded off its hinges and slammed into the opposite wall.

Pierce whirled and leapt across the short distance to the open office where Nina urged him on. As soon as he was through, she slammed the door behind him.

Pierce saw that they were in a lunchroom. The two tables and a scattering of chairs offered nothing in the way of a hiding place, but he saw a way to put the refrigerator against one wall to use. Nina divined his intent, and working together they quickly rolled the heavy appliance across the floor and positioned it in front of the door.

"That's not going to stop them," Nina warned.

"I know." He scanned the room again, looking for anything that might help them survive the assault. He dashed over to the sink counter and yanked open the cupboard. The space was occupied by a small refuse can and a few bottles of cleaning supplies, but he saw that there might be room for a person of slight build to hide there. He cleared the area out with a sweep of his hand. "Hide in here."

"What about you?"

"Just do it. I'll think of something."

Her eyes widened as she realized the sacrifice he was preparing to make, but she complied, squirming into the cramped cupboard. "Good luck," she whispered as he closed the cabinet doors, sealing her in.

Pierce knew luck was about the only thing that would save him, and the sudden pounding from behind the refrigerator blocking the exit door indicated that his luck had run out.

He scanned the room again, then started opening cupboards and drawers, looking for anything that might be useful in warding off the impending assault. Aside from the tables and chairs, the only things he saw were a small microwave oven, a toaster and a case of bottled water on the counter, along with an honor jar filled with loose change. In one drawer, mixed in with an array of spoons and spatulas, he found a long knife with a serrated edge, but the idea of using it against the monsters seemed laughable.

The refrigerator jumped a few feet away from door, and Pierce instinctively rushed to it, and made a futile effort to brace it with his shoulder. He managed to push it forward a few inches, but then something hit it again from behind, and knocked him back. He fell into one of the tables, banging his hip painfully on one edge, and went sprawling onto the floor.

Wincing from the bruising injury, he rolled over just in time to see one of the hair-cloaked creatures advance into the room. Its red eyes met his gaze, and with a nerve-shattering scream, it started toward him.

36.

King knew that Sokoloff was now the least of his worries.

Copeland had been overly optimistic in his belief that the Army could hold off the assault for eight minutes. According to his still running chronometer, only about six minutes had passed since the activation of the Bluelight device—six minutes in which the creatures had seemingly materialized out of the mist and managed to either find a break in the perimeter or completely overrun the soldiers. And now, the only person who could have stopped it all by shutting down the experiment was dead.

And that wasn't even the worst of it.

Eight and a half minutes is the upper limit of the green zone, Copeland had said. In his mind's eye, he saw a temperature gauge with green, yellow and red segments. The imaginary needle was almost out of the green now, advancing relentlessly toward yellow and red. In perhaps in as little as five more minutes, the antimatter explosions in the Earth's magnetic field would grow hot enough to set the world on fire, and there was no way to shut it off.

But there's got to be a way to stop it, King thought.

He couldn't tell if the creatures that now flooded into the control room were actively looking for him or just destroying everything in sight, but either way, he only had a few more seconds before they found him, crouched beneath a flimsy computer desk. King decided not to postpone the inevitable any longer.

He scrambled out of concealment, taking in the room like a game board, with the towering Mogollon Monsters arrayed like enemy pieces, blocking his path to the objective. He didn't see Sokoloff, and entertained a fleeting hope that the beasts had already taken care of that little problem. Taking a deep breath, he hurled a chair at one of the creatures, hoping to distract it more than anything else, and then launched himself in a low sprint for the exit.

A sweeping arm grazed him, knocking him off course, but he rebounded off the doorframe and scrambled into the darkened foyer. The door to the outside had been completely torn away, and beyond it, the world strobed between night and day as lightning—or rather charged plasma from the atmosphere—flashed like the cameras of a dozen crazed paparazzi on the red carpet. The frequency of the flashes was increasing, with several flashes per second, and the constant roar of thunder resonated through King's torso like the mother of all woofers.

He burst out into the open, slowing only long enough to take in the carnage. The soldiers hadn't been completely annihilated, but the few remaining survivors were clustered around a Humvee to his right, fiercely repelling more than a dozen monsters. Their battle was drawing more creatures in like the gravity well of a black hole. The area to his right was eerily deserted, with wrecked and abandoned Humvees jutting up out of the waist high mist. King swerved in that direction and resumed running, staying close to the exterior of the building.

As he rounded the corner, he was exposed to the full fury of the artificial lightning storm.

The air was alive with heat and electricity. He could feel the static crawling on his skin as he raced along the side of the building, toward the precipice overlooking the abandoned pit mine. The mist hid the exact location of the drop, but as he neared the place where the silvery fog seemed to cascade out into nothingness, he cautiously tested the ground before each step, getting as close as he dared.

There, at the edge of the vast manmade crater, he got his first look at the Bluelight device.

The actual structure was unremarkable. It didn't look much different than an oil rig or an industrial manufacturing facility. At its center, perhaps half a mile away, and several hundred feet below on the floor of the pit, was an upright column, similar to the cooling tower of a nuclear power plant, surrounded by catwalks and miles of wires and tubing. King assumed that the column was heart of Bluelight, the proton gun that was currently firing a steady stream of subatomic particles into the sky, but if the discharge was accompanied by any sort of visible effect, it was impossible to see against the arc-welder bright flashes of lightning. The plasma bursts were being gathered by three metal towers that looked like radio transmitter aerials, each taller than the proton emitter, positioned as points of a triangle around the center.

As he gazed out across the pit, King's hopes of somehow reaching the Bluelight device and shutting it down manually evaporated. Even if he somehow found a way down to the floor of the mine—a journey that would almost certainly take longer than the few minutes remaining until the world caught fire—the energies being pulled down from the sky would incinerate him long before he reached it. It was all he could do to endure the blisteringly hot fury of the storm here, at the edge of the pit.

But then he glimpsed something that wasn't quite so far away. Directly below, at the base of the sheer wall, was another familiar looking structure, one that could be found in any American city: an electrical transformer station.

Bluelight pulled massive amounts of raw energy from the sky, but for its own operation, it needed a steady, measured flow of electricity. Copeland and Mayfield had talked about how the device would be used to charge storage batteries; the transformer was a critical step in that process.

Destroy the transformer, and Bluelight goes dark, King thought.

The transformer was almost as unreachable as Bluelight itself, but as he shaded his eyes with one hand, peering down the side of the pit, King saw the solution and felt a fleeting instant of hope.

But as he turned around to carry out his desperate plan, something slammed into the side of his head and sent him sprawling toward the precipice.

37.

Pierce stared up at the beast, searching for some trace of the humanity he had glimpsed during his sojourn into the underworld, but it simply wasn't there. The creature's eyes might have been the color of fresh blood, but the real thing was dripping from its bared teeth and oozing from dozens of wounds on its body to splatter onto the floor.

Then he glimpsed something familiar. Dangling from a string around the monster's neck was a dark, discolored coin with the distinctive likeness of the goddess Athena. The *tetradrachm*. This was the same creature that had attacked the motorist. The coin it wore as a totem was the very thing that had drawn him into this nightmare.

He wasn't sure if that met the definition of irony, but the realization was bitter nonetheless.

The thing howled again, spraying Pierce with bloody spittle. Almost overwhelmed by its pungent odor, the archaeologist crab-walked backward, scrambling to put some distance between himself and the creature, desperate to postpone the inevitable, if only for a few seconds longer. The monster lurched forward, and despite the fact that there was nowhere to go, Pierce turned and ran.

Even though he barely knew her, he had a sudden urge to protect Nina. He angled away from the sink cabinet where she hid and skirted the counter, hoping to draw the creature after him and possibly lure it out of the room. But as he reached the corner, his eyes lit on something, and a light bulb of crazy inspiration flashed on in his head.

As he rounded the corner, still trying to stay ahead of the monster's extraordinarily long reach, he snatched up the jar from beside the case of bottled water and ripped the lid off. Whispering the quickest prayer he could remember, he thrust his hand in and spun around, holding up the object that he hoped would save him: a United States quarter-dollar coin. He was betting his life against twenty-five cents.

The creature stopped abruptly right in front of him, with both arms spread wide, as if intended to sweep him into a crushing embrace. Pierce kept his hand extended, but closed his eyes in anticipation of the end.

All he could hear was the rasp of the monster's breathing, and after a few seconds—seconds in which he did not have the life squeezed out of him—he risked a look.

The creature was still there, right in front of him. Its eyes were still blazing with crimson fury. Its teeth were still bared in a grimace of rage. But it hadn't killed him.

That was a good sign.

The monster slowly lowered its arms, and then reached out to him. Pierce felt its fingers brush his as it plucked the offering from his grasp. The tiny metal disc vanished in its hairy fist, but it drew back its arms with an almost reverent air. With its free hand, the beast plucked the totem string from around its neck and lowered it over Pierce's head. Then, as if it satisfied with the exchange, it turned and stalked out of the room.

Pierce gasped as he realized he had been holding his breath, and then sagged to his knees. His fingers brushed against the silver *obol* coin the creature had given him. He'd definitely come out ahead on the trade.

38.

King threw his arms out, scrabbling for something to hang onto even as he felt the ground fall away from under his legs. He'd taken more than his share of shots to the cranium and knew how to deal with the momentary disorientation that followed, but hanging from the edge of a cliff with searing heat and lighting buffeting his back was a lot different than trying to get back up off the mat before the ten-count was finished. One wrong move here, one hand in the wrong place or his weight shifted in the wrong direction, and he'd get a very close, very brief look at the transformer station.

The mist hid everything from him, including the face of his attacker, but he had caught a glimpse in the instant before the attack. *Sokoloff.* Well, better the Russian hitman than a mob of Mogollon Monsters.

King's lower torso and legs were hanging out into no-thingness, and he felt the hard edge of the pit pressing into his abdomen just below his rib cage. He pressed himself flat against the rough rock and began working his way forward. If he could get just a few more inches of his body back onto solid ground, he'd be home free...relatively speaking. But every inch took a few seconds, and he was all too conscious of the fact that each second he spent trying to pull himself back onto solid ground brought the world that much closer to destruction.

Then Sokoloff did him a favor.

He heard a scratching sound and saw something move in the mist right in front of him, close enough that he could see a military-issue boot probing the ground for solidity.

King grabbed the ankle with both hands and tried to heave himself up and out of the pit. The maneuver was only partly successful. Sokoloff's weight rested on his back foot and when King pulled, he felt the Russian shift backward in an effort to keep his balance. The attempt failed and Sokoloff's other foot went out from under him. As King tried to pull himself up, he succeeded only in pulling the Russian closer to the edge, and in the process, he lost what little progress he had made and then some.

Somehow, Sokoloff arrested his slide. King kept his death grip on the hitman's ankle and hauled in again. A swirling in the mist warned him that something was moving and he lowered his head as Sokoloff's other boot struck out at him. The heel glanced off the side of his head and hammered into his shoulder. Before the Russian could draw back for another kick, King released one hand and snared the other foot. With a mighty heave, he hauled himself away from the edge and rolled sideways into the embrace of the mist.

"I see now why you're worth ten million dollars, King." The Russian's voice reached out to him, shouting to be audible over the thunder.

"Ten million?" King managed to sound more confident than he felt. His head was throbbing from the blows he'd sustained, and the constant sonic bombardment was like a meat tenderizer working on his muscles. "Is that all Brainstorm thinks I'm worth? No wonder he can only afford cheap-ass punks like you."

"Ha. What is it you Americans say? 'Big talk is cheap'? I have killed six hundred and eighty-four men. Five of them, your vaunted airborne infantry, this very night. How many have you killed?"

King cocked his head, trying to pinpoint Sokoloff's location from his shouted boasts. He got to hands and knees, and then lifted his head up for a quick peek, but the Russian was staying low as well, lurking beneath the mist like a shark in the shallows.

You're not the only shark in the pool tonight, Ivan.

"Guess I never kept track," King called out. "But whatever it is, it's going to be plus one in a few minutes."

He rolled back toward the cliff, going to what he hoped was the last place the hitman would expect, then low crawled as quietly as possible along the edge...ten meters...twenty. A ripple in the mist cover alerted him to danger and he rolled to the side as the long blade of a combat knife flashed out and stabbed down at him. The tip scored his back, opening a long but superficial gash, before striking the rock where he had been only an instant before.

King reversed and threw himself onto the hand that held the knife, pinning it to the ground, even as he reached out to grapple with its wielder. He was close enough to see his opponent; Sokoloff still wore the uniform and equipment of the soldier whose identity he had assumed, and while the bulky armor was a liability in terms of mobility, it limited King's ability to find a vulnerable spot to focus his attack. The Russian struggled against him, and King felt the arm that held the knife start to move, warning of another thrust. He threw one arm up to ward off the blow, and then wrapped the other around the hitman's helmeted head.

Levering his body like an Olympic weightlifter, he wrenched the helmet around, as if trying to twist Sokoloff's head off his shoulders. He succeeded only in tearing the helmet free, and rolled away with the Kevlar composite shell clutched in his hand.

Sokoloff roared in agony as his neck twisted and the nylon straps ripped away skin, but his rage fueled a swift recovery and he slashed at King with his knife. King parried with the helmet, knocking the knife hand away with a solid blow, and then in the same motion, backhanded Sokoloff's exposed jaw.

The Russian's head snapped back as the helmet demolished bone and teeth. He flailed his arms, dazed, but King pressed the attack, slamming the combat helmet into the hitman's skull. As the dazed man stumbled, King moved in to finish things quick and clean. He caught the man's head in his hands and with a quick twist, broke the assassin's neck. The man slumped to the ground at King's feet.

There was no time to savor the victory however, or even to catch his breath. It had been just over ten minutes since the Bluelight device's activation. King had no idea how much longer the world had to live, but he was pretty sure the needle was now well into the red.

39.

With the fury of the storm at his back, King ran. He rounded the corner of the building and saw the last remaining soldiers swinging their spent carbines like clubs, trying in vain to beat back the growing mass of attacking Mogollon Monsters. He felt a pang at witnessing their plight, but there was only one way to help them, and it didn't involve joining the fray.

As he ran for the nearest Humvee that was still upright, several of the creatures took note of his presence and started loping toward him. The M1026 had been battered relentlessly. All the doors had been ripped off their hinges and the aluminum shell was crumpled like a discarded beer can, but King leapt into the misshapen cab and started the engine. One of the thick-skinned creatures got a hand on the vehicle as he punched the accelerator, but the spinning tires threw up a spray of gravel that knocked it back.

He steered straight out onto open ground, away from the Bluelight facility and the shifting horde, letting the vehicle build up some momentum. When the speedometer needle registered forty miles per hour, he carved a wide turn and brought the truck around, lining up parallel to the side of the concrete structure and pointing straight into the heart of the electrical storm. His detour out into the desert had put about a quarter of a mile between him and his ultimate destination; the Humvee would close that distance in about twenty seconds.

He reached under the steering wheel and found the hand-throttle control that was intended to be used with the vehicle's self-recovery winch. Every Humvee with a winch had a manual throttle, as well as a prominently displayed, printed message stating that it was not to be used as a cruise control. The reason was that unlike sophisticated cruise-control systems, the hand-throttle would not switch off when the brakes were applied.

King had no intention of braking.

He pulled the knob completely out, opening the throttle wide, just as the corner of the building flashed by, then immediately launched himself from the speeding vehicle. Much like the Humvee, King was on autopilot. He knew what had to be done, and he didn't allow himself to think about the consequences. Thinking would lead to hesitation, and if he had hesitated even a moment in making his leap, he probably wouldn't have made it out in time. He'd jumped out of too many airplanes to count, and between a youth spent riding skateboards and motorcycling in later years, he'd torn himself up on pavement more than a few times. His body knew what to do, and as he pushed away from the truck, he let muscle memory take over.

His muscles might have remembered what to do, but his body had definitely forgotten about what it would feel like. The silvery mist looked deceptively soft as he jumped, but it simply swirled out of the way as he passed through, traveling at fifty miles an hour. He did his best to curl into a ball, tucking his head against his chest and drawing his arms and legs close to his body, but when he hit the hard rocky ground, any semblance of control went out the window.

The next few moments were a blur of pain and motion, but through the relentless pummeling and the abrasive scraping, he remembered that there was a cliff ahead, and he tried to extend his extremities spread-eagle to slow his doomward slide.

It must have worked, because after a few more tumbles, he came to rest, shrouded in mist. He was almost grateful for the pain, because it told him he was still alive.

40.

King didn't get to see the Humvee finish its short unmanned trip. While he was still tumbling, the military vehicle shot past the edge of the crater and sailed out over the mine. It nosed over at the end of the short parabolic arc and plummeted straight down. Deprived of all resistance, the engine revved loudly, spinning the wheels even faster, but it was gravity—not diesel fuel—that increased the truck's speed, albeit only for about three seconds. Then, it came to a very sudden stop.

The Humvee slammed into the middle of the transformer station, annihilating the electrical equipment with kinetic energy alone. The truck then exploded in a ball of fire and debris that finished the job.

As spectacular as the explosion was, it paled alongside the amount of raw power raining down from the sky. And even though the destruction of the transformer instantly shut down the electricity supply to the proton emitter, the storm caused by the anti-matter annihilation in the upper atmosphere did not immediately abate. The lightning continued to hammer down into the collection towers, and because the mechanism for drawing the energy away had been destroyed, the plasma simply pooled at the base of the aerial structures.

In a matter of only a few seconds, the floor of the mine grew hotter than the surface of the sun. Solid matter—steel, copper, concrete, even a layer of rock some thirty feet thick—instantly flashed into plasma, as Bluelight became a flash of pure white light.

EPILOGUE

1044 UTC (3:44 am Local)

The pain might have been proof that he had survived the tumble from the Humvee, but it wasn't until the mist receded—almost as if sucked back into the Earth—revealing a dark sky, speckled with stars, that King knew his plan had worked.

He got gingerly to his feet, and hesitantly checked himself for damage. All things considered, he'd come out of it pretty well. There were a couple of threadbare spots on his jeans, dark with blood oozing from abrasions underneath, but they were mostly intact. The same could not be said for his favorite Elvis shirt, which hung in shreds from his shoulders. Surprisingly, despite a full body tattoo of scrapes and bruises, the only significant injury he'd sustained was the shallow gash across his back, courtesy of Sokoloff's knife.

More or less steady on his feet, he ambled forward to the now visible precipice, and stared out into the dark crater where Bluelight had stood only a few moments before.

There was a sharp odor of burning metal, but the air above the pit was clear. The floor of the mine crater was dark, and

King could only make out a faint glow, like the belly of a red hot woodstove, several hundred feet below. Aside from that, there was no visible sign that Bluelight had ever existed.

There was gasp from behind him. "Oh my God."

King turned to find Pierce and Nina, both seemingly stunned into paralysis by his appearance. He rushed to them and swept them both into his embrace. "You made it. I didn't think anyone…" He let go of the pair and took a step back. "The Muggy Monsters? Are they still…?"

Nina shook her head. "All gone. They left with the mist. Took all the dead with them."

King nodded slowly. All the dead. Soldiers and fallen creatures alike. King had managed to save the world, but Bluelight's promised "free energy" had come at enormous cost.

"They're still out there," Pierce said. "Or I should say 'under.' But without that machine to drive them crazy, I think our war with the underworld has entered a ceasefire."

"I see you picked up a souvenir." King tapped the coin, hanging around Pierce's neck.

"Yeah. Long story. I'll tell you about it when we're somewhere that isn't here." Pierce managed a grim smile. "Jack, you look like shit."

"You should see the other guy. Speaking of which…" King glanced around and spied a body that had evidently escaped the notice of the retreating Mogollon Monsters. Sokoloff lay where he had fallen, only a few feet from the edge of the cliff.

Ten million dollars, King thought. *That's what Brainstorm offered him to take me down.*

Had Brainstorm known that he would be drawn to Bluelight? Or had the death bounty been placed merely as an act of revenge for thwarting Brainstorm's earlier schemes? Either way, King knew that taking down Brainstorm was no longer going to be merely a side project.

King's phone suddenly chirped a familiar ringtone. He pulled it out, shocked that the thing still worked at all, and answered. "Aleman?"

"Guess again," came Deep Blue's voice. "What's your sit rep?"

"Things got a little…hairy, but we're okay now. Situation is contained. By the way, this wasn't a Manifold project, it was Brainstorm. Again. I'll give you my full report when I get back."

"Sounds good," Deep Blue said. "Just make sure you're long gone by the time Army reinforcements roll in. The fewer questions we have to answer, the better. I'll make sure the right people get your intel."

King knew that the "right people" were Domenick Boucher, director of the CIA and Deep Blue's trusted friend, and General Micheal Keasling, who the team had served under while officially part of Delta. They would know how to disseminate the intel.

"So where were you?" King asked, curious about what had pulled the man away from setting up their new headquarters in New Hampshire.

Deep Blue laughed. "I," he said, "was picking up Fiona. She had a camping trip sprung on her and after a few hours in the dark, decided she wanted to come home. She was near tears when she called. Asked me not to tell you about it, but well, sharing secrets with each other is part of our jobs."

Fiona was sometimes plagued by nightmares of monsters and stone giants. She was a tough kid, but even the most battle-hardened soldier was sometimes haunted by a touch of post-traumatic stress. That she'd been shanghaied into a camping trip made King angry, but he was glad she felt confident enough to have the former President of the United States come to her rescue. "Next time we'll trade missions," King said. "I'll pick up my kid. *You* can deal with the monsters."

When King hung up the phone, he found Nina smiling at him. "*You* have a kid?"

King smiled, thinking about how nice it would be to see Fiona. "In fact, I do."

The conversation was interrupted by a familiar buzzing noise. He looked down at the phone in his hand. The cracked screen was blank. The hum repeated...from Sokoloff's body.

King rifled through the man's pockets until he found the Russian's phone. He tapped the screen to display the message:

Status report requested.

King realized that he held in his hand a direct link to Brainstorm. One of the oldest maxims of war was: "Know your enemy," but King knew nothing about Brainstorm. Was it, as Deep Blue had speculated, an artificially intelligent computer network? Or was it just an ordinary human with extraordinary resources and an ego to match? Sokoloff's phone was a loose thread on the curtain behind which Brainstorm hid. It was time to pull that thread.

He quickly scrolled through the archive of messages between the hitman and his employer. Sokoloff's relationship with Brainstorm went back several weeks. There was no way that the contract could be tied to a desire to protect Bluelight, since that problem hadn't even been recognized until much later. That meant it was personal; Brainstorm was afraid of King.

It was all there: the plot to use Pierce to lure King into the open, instructions on where to acquire equipment, bank account information and of course, the most important thing, a direct number that led to Brainstorm...or would at least, until it became apparent that the assassin had failed.

Time to strike the first blow, King thought.

He tapped out a reply:

It's done. King is dead.

ABOUT THE AUTHORS

JEREMY ROBINSON is the author of eleven novels including PULSE, INSTINCT, and THRESHOLD the first three books in his exciting Jack Sigler series. His novels have been translated into nine languages. He is also the director of New Hampshire AuthorFest, a non-profit organization promoting literacy. He lives in New Hampshire with his wife and three children.

Visit him on the web, here:
www.jeremyrobinsononline.com

SEAN ELLIS is the author of several novels. He is a veteran of Operation Enduring Freedom, and has a Bachelor of Science degree in Natural Resources Policy from Oregon State University. He lives in Arizona, where he divides his time between writing, adventure sports, and trying to figure out how to save the world.

Visit him on the web, here:
seanellisthrillers.webs.com

ALSO IN 2011

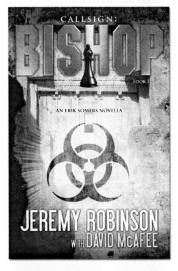

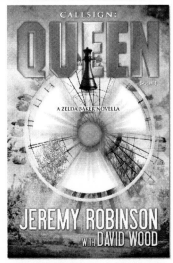

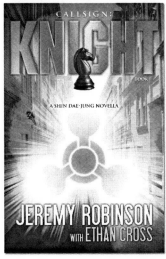

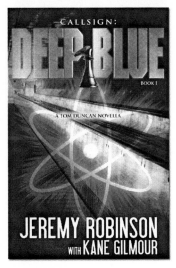

CPSIA information can be obtained at www.ICGtesting.com
Printed in the USA
LVOW041548301111

257171LV00003B/2/P